# LESSONS IN SURVIVAL:
# ALL ABOUT AMOS

# Lessons in Survival: All About Amos

A novel
by

## SUSAN L. POLLET

Adelaide Books
New York/Lisbon
2019

LESSONS IN SURVIVAL: ALL ABOUT AMOS
A novel
By Susan L. Pollet

Copyright © by Susan L. Pollet
Cover design © 2019 Adelaide Books
Cover image: Susan L. Pollet


Published by Adelaide Books, New York / Lisbon
adelaidebooks.org
Editor-in-Chief
Stevan V. Nikolic

For any information, please address Adelaide Books
at info@adelaidebooks.org
or write to:
Adelaide Books
244 Fifth Ave. Suite D27
New York, NY, 10001


ISBN-10: 1-949180-90-5
ISBN-13: 978-1-949180-90-9


Printed in the United States of America

# Contents

*There are those who turn justice into bitterness and cast*

*righteousness to the ground. Amos 5:7*

*But not this Amos.*

# *Prologue*

If you are fortunate, you will meet someone who inspires you in your life. In case you have not, or need more uplifting, I am sharing Amos's story with you for whatever lessons and motivations you can draw from it. The bare outlines of his story are not unique in that he is the son of parents who were Holocaust survivors and who both lost their families. The fact that he was born in Israel and raised as a Jew from the age of three in post World War II Cologne, Germany is unusual. More importantly, the way in which he dealt with his family's dark and tragic history is original to him and reflects his strong spirit. He made an art of learning to survive, thrive, and of never succumbing to bitterness.

Born in Haifa, Israel, raised in post World War II Germany with his sister under difficult financial circumstances and with parents who suffered the effects of having been in concentration camps, he managed to succeed despite having been the only Jewish boy in his school classes amongst seven hundred students. He took care of his family on a practical level from a very early age-the classic parentified child. He eventually went to medical school in Germany and then moved to New York City for his medical residency, where he remained. When I met Amos in New York City, he had two board certifications, he was an obstetrician and gynecologist, a specialist in maternal-fetal medicine, and a professor at a major medical institution; he lectured throughout the world; he was a published author of numerous peer reviewed journals and a few popular books; he had developed several patents; he was an entrepreneur-the creator and operator of a major medical website (and had previously sold two other websites); and he was an outstanding photographer, along with many other accomplishments including fluency in three languages and advanced cooking skills. He had lived through two failed marriages; he had one child of his first marriage; he had suffered a stroke in his late forties, and again in his sixties, and survived cancer, heart attacks, several abdominal surgeries, and other serious medical challenges. He stood five feet, six inches tall, spoke with a heavy German accent, maintained a confident swagger, had boundless energy, a twinkle in his blue eyes, and mischief in his personality. He was and is a force to be reckoned with.

Soon after I met Amos, with tears in his eyes and deep emotion, he showed me boxes full of photographs of his family, and other memorabilia, and, over the years, regaled me with stories of his life, which I began to record. He told me that the biggest influences on his life were his parents and another doctor, his Chairman, with whom he worked for many years. When he met people, even for the first time, he would tell them some of these family stories, which on occasion, before the wrong audience, could be too much information. I concluded that this was his way of connecting and letting people know who he was and is. It was as if he did not want anybody whom he encountered to forget what happened to his parents and, by extension, what happened to him.

When interviewing Amos for this book, there were certain challenges. One of his survival traits, which he learned from his parents, was to fail to remember psychological issues, and to tell himself white lies in order to cope with some very difficult experiences, so I cannot swear to total accuracy as to the original stories, his recounting of what happened, or in my interpretation of them. His disassociation or lack of self-awareness even went to such an extreme that he did not know he had blue eyes. And yet because of his absolute intellectual brilliance, and the wide range of subjects he could embrace, there is enough here for you to draw your own conclusions, and, perhaps, to learn how to have his swagger. He does not want anyone to forget what happened to his family, and I want people to know how he has prevailed. Perhaps in understanding the essence of his soul, and reflecting how it came to be, I am able to best express this love poem and tribute to him and to his family.

# Chapter One: Rachel

*"Pray that you will never have to bear all
that you are able to endure"*

—Jewish Proverb

From everything I was able to learn, Amos is most like his mother Rachel, now deceased, in that he has her finely chiseled features, her generous nature, her ability to nurture and to see life in an upbeat way, her resilience, and the ability to cook well as a form of love. To understand Rachel's background is to understand Amos. They shared a special, close bond, and Amos had only the most positive things to say about her. It is almost as if any criticism of her would be sinful given all that she endured in her life. He blocked out anything negative about her. What is undeniable is that he felt truly loved by her. He, in fact, took more care of her throughout his life than the reverse although he never expressed even the slightest hint of resentment for it. He had compassion and a profound sense of duty toward her to make her life better than it had been.

Amos did not remember exactly when he learned all of these stories about his mother, but he recalled that she did not tell him much until he was a teenager. At other times Amos said that his parents talked about the war every day in their home. His sister recalled being told much more on a daily basis from the time she was six years of age, and that their mother would always answer her inquiries. It was not until Amos was in his forties that he learned one terrible secret that Rachel had kept from him for nearly five decades, which was that Amos had another sister whose name he does not know and whom he has never met. The traumas his parents suffered were felt by the entire family, although Amos denied that they had any negative effect on him. Both Amos and his sister had difficulty remembering details of what they were told, which is apparently common for second generation Holocaust survivor families. Although Rachel's life story was recorded by the Shoah Visual History Foundation founded by the film director, Steven Spielberg, Amos could not bear to watch her recording, and has not to this day. It is too painful for him. He also refused to watch any movies or read any books about the Holocaust, and gets upset if he starts to. His overpowering empathy created this reaction.

Rachel was born on December 9, 1923 in Sighet, Romania as the ninth and youngest child of a famous Hasidic family, known for its' Rabbis. One child had died. Rachel's mother was approximately forty years of age when Rachel was born. Several of Rachel's eldest sisters and brothers were already married and had children. Rachel described herself to Amos as a rebel and black sheep because she did not embrace the orthodox traditions of her family and community. Two thirds of the population in Sighet was Jewish and adhered to these traditions. She always questioned why she had to comply with what she considered to be arbitrary and nonsensical rules. For example, one was not permitted to make fires or to turn lights on or off on Shabbat. When the Jewish families went to bed on Friday evening, someone would step out into the street to find a non-Jewish person to put out the lights. They were called Shabbos goys. Rachel wanted to turn the lights out herself, which upset her parents. She could never understand the culture and never wavered in her belief that the rules made no sense. She would open the door on Friday evenings, pretend to ask someone to turn out the lights, do it herself, and then thank the air in a loud voice. She was not permitted to go to the cinema, but she did so anyway. On one occasion, one of her sisters waited outside the cinema when she came out. After that she had trouble at home and was not permitted to attend again. The restrictions on her freedom felt intolerable to her.

At the age of eighteen or nineteen, the young women in that community would be married off. There was a woman, a matchmaker, who brought several young men to Rachel's home in order to make a marital arrangement, but Rachel refused every young boy who came there. This caused a lot of trouble for her with her parents.

Rachel's parents owned a restaurant which served Kosher food, and she lived and worked there during the week and ate her lunch and dinner there. In order to remain true to Jewish laws about working on the Sabbath, every Friday afternoon her father sold the restaurant to a non-Jewish employee for a nominal fee who took care of the restaurant until Saturday evening when her father bought it back. Her mother took care of the money and was the cashier. Her brothers were educated at a Jewish school and her father learned in the shul, the synagogue. Before Rachel was born, her sisters obtained what was then considered a good education for girls with a private teacher in the house. They learned German, Romanian, Hungarian, Hebrew, and sewing. As Rachel was the last child, no one really took care of her or educated her, and she went to school only until age ten. In addition to working at the restaurant, an Aunt showed her how to make dresses, and she became a seamstress. Despite having received little formal education, at the time of her death at age 86, she could read, write and speak in six languages, and was proficient at using the computer.

Rachel and her youngest brother were the only ones living in the house with their parents when she was in her late teens. Some of her siblings went to Palestine before the war as they were Zionists. One sibling went to the United States. One sister and one brother went to a town in Romania where the Germans did not invade and so they survived. Rachel continued to refuse to marry. At the time of the war, her father considered himself to be a Hungarian and not a Romanian. He believed that the Romanians were not as intelligent. The family spoke Yiddish and Hungarian at home, while Romanian was spoken in the schools. Initially Rachel's father was pleased when the Hungarian troops "liberated" Sighet from Romanian rule. When Rachel's father found out that the Hungarians were working with the Germans, and that the Germans had come to Sighet, he was extremely upset. The family speculated that this was the reason that he had a heart attack and died. Their restaurant closed as there were restrictions on businesses run by Jews.

In 1940, the army of what was then Hungary invaded the north-west portion of Romania, including Sighet, which was also known as Transylvania. The Jews were placed into ghettos, including Rachel and her mother. Each family took a suitcase. When they moved to the ghetto, they shared a small one bedroom apartment. There was no indoor plumbing. They lived in that apartment for about a year. The Germans came closer and closer, and the Hungarians took over.

Some time after the invasion, but prior to her going into the ghetto, Rachel's home was partially occupied by German soldiers. Rachel was very beautiful, and was the only sister who was not married. A blonde, tall German soldier, who was living in her home, befriended her. He told her that terrible things would happen to the Jews and that he would help her to flee into the part of Romania which was not occupied by the Hungarians or the Germans. Rachel did not believe that such things could happen and did not take him up on his offer. Around the same time, a Jewish man arrived in the village and went to the synagogue. He told people that there were camps outside Transylvania where Jews were being killed and starved to death. The Jews in Sighet did not believe him. They thought he was mentally ill and admitted him to an insane asylum.

When Rachel and her mother moved into the ghetto, they lived with a remote relative with seven people in one room. The relative was a farmer, he had a cow, and there was always a bit to eat. Rachel worked at a hospital in the ghetto. She did whatever work was necessary to keep the hospital clean and to take care of the patients. For that work, she received extra food. Nobody was hungry then, and nobody felt in danger. Perhaps Amos's choice to become a doctor was influenced by his mother's stories of her life.

One day in May, 1944, the German and Hungarian authorities told the Jews in the Sighet ghetto that they would be relocated and would be allowed to take a small amount of belongings with them. Rachel's family had Shabbat candles and some silver for the holy days. Rachel gave the precious family items in a suitcase to non-Jewish neighbors to hold until she returned. When Rachel returned after the war, those neighbors could not remember that she had given them those items.

About 15,000 people over a three day period were assembled at the train station. They were herded into cattle cars. Over 400,000 Jews were deported by Hungarians and

Germans to the concentration camp, Auschwitz-Birkenau. Most of the mothers, children and elderly were immediately gassed upon arriving there.

Rachel and her family were transported on the third train to Auschwitz-Birkenau. The famous author, Elie Wiesel, grew up with Rachel in Sighet, and was in the transport with her. She was also with three of her sisters, her mother, and approximately fifteen nieces and nephews, who were her sisters' children.

They spent three days in the cattle cars while being transported, with very little food or water and no bathroom facilities. They used a bucket to urinate in. These train cars had previously been used to transport animals. There were no windows. The men and women separated themselves, and put up a blanket to divide the space for privacy. The car was full such that it was not big enough for everyone to sit on the floor.

When the train occasionally stopped, the passengers would knock on the door and scream. Sometimes they were allowed to empty the bucket. They were not permitted to leave the cars. The smell of bodies and desperation were unbearable for Rachel. She described this to Amos, and it haunts him. But, as all students of history know, this was just the beginning.

When they arrived at the concentration camp, they were told to disembark. The German soldiers ordered the men and women to line up separately. The soldiers had German Shepherd dogs with them. There is a photograph of Rachel in that line, which was later found by Amos's relatives in an historical book, and given to him. Amos saw that same photograph hanging in a museum in Prague seventy years after the event. He was not expecting to see it there. His mother's tongue was out, pointed in the direction of the German soldiers. She was a rebel even then, not truly appreciating the dangers that awaited her.

The selection process began. Rachel, who was not married, was carrying two children of one of her sisters. Rachel's mother, her sisters and the children were sent in one direction, as was Rachel. She walked with them in that direction. She was stopped shortly afterwards by a man in an SS uniform who asked her whether the children belonged to her. She later learned that the man was Josef Mengele, the infamous German Schutzstaffel officer and physician in Auschwitz. Rachel said that they were her sister's children. The SS soldier told Rachel to give the children to their mother, and he sent Rachel in a different direction. Rachel asked why her family was going in a different direction, and the SS soldier told her that older women and mothers with children would be provided with transportation. Rachel was upset because she had to walk several miles without the other members of her family. Rachel's mother's last words to her were to always be faithful and to believe in God.

The day Rachel arrived at the camp, she was brought into the showers with other women. It was especially embarrassing for unmarried, young Hasidic girls to be naked in such a setting, and Rachel felt that keenly. Her entire body was shaved, and she was showered and deloused. Chemicals were showered upon her. She was then given a gray dress, wooden shoes, underwear, and no bra. She was wearing the same dress, underwear and shoes eleven months later when she was rescued, without them ever having been washed.

Rachel was brought into a barrack. She had to share a bed with eight other people without blankets or mattresses, only hay. There were three levels of bunk beds, with nine people in each rectangular box. She could not lay down in the box. There were hundreds of people in each room. When she woke up the next morning, she asked another woman who had been at the camp for a while where her mother was taken. The woman pointed through the window to a chimney, with smoke coming out of it. She told Rachel "that is where your mother is right now." Rachel thought she was insane. It took her several days to realize that her family had been cremated. She was unable to conceive that people could be capable of doing these things to others.

She spent the next six weeks in Birkenau. They received food only once a day, which consisted of watery soup. They were permitted to use the communal bathrooms, also only once a day. There were about fifty toilet seats in a row. They were allowed to spend a couple of minutes sitting on the toilet seats. A woman walked behind them with sticks. She beat them when it was time for them to get up. Meanwhile, the soldiers were inside watching. Rachel had trouble with constipation for her entire life because of this experience. There were communal sinks and tiled walls with built in soap dishes. Rachel felt acutely the irony of fancy soap dishes in this place of torture. When Amos visited the camp with Rachel many years later, they took one of the soap dishes, without hesitation. Rachel wanted Amos to have a reminder that what she had been describing to him for many years had really happened to her.

Rachel and the others had to stand in attendance once in the morning and once in the evening. They were counted and the soldiers looked carefully at each of them. Whenever one of the women seemed to be sick, she was taken away and no one saw her again. It was only later that Rachel and the others learned that these women were taken to the gas chamber. The women would make themselves look healthy by pinching their cheeks to look slightly red. When Rachel was taking a shower on the wooden floor when she first arrived, she got a splinter on her foot, which was full of pus afterwards. Even though it hurt her badly, she hid it. She knew that if the soldiers saw it, she would be taken to the gas chamber. In order to survive there, she quickly learned that if she got injured or sick, or if she was imperfect in some way, she would have to hide it or be killed. She felt herself to be "a person without a brain." She could not think or decide anything, and some of the other women took care of her.

Most of the women in Birkenau received a tattoo with a number, but Rachel did not. Rachel's explanation to Amos for this was that she was not a person worth the ink because they did not know if they wanted to keep her alive or not.

About six weeks after her arrival, the concentration camp inmates were ordered to report at the square. The soldiers announced that they were permitted to volunteer for a work assignment which would provide better food and working conditions. There was a lot of confusion among the girls because they did not know if this was a trick, or if it would be an actual improvement of their situation. They ran back and forth to one another. Some girls who had decided to volunteer tried to convince those who did not want to volunteer that this was their best chance at survival. Other girls who had decided not to volunteer screamed at the others that this was just a trap. Rachel decided that nothing could be worse than what she had experienced the preceding six weeks. She decided to volunteer along with a pair of siblings who were her friends.

Approximately 1200 girls volunteered for the work assignment, and were chosen. The girls, including Rachel, were brought into trains and transported to Essen, Germany to the Krupps factory which manufactured weapons for the war. Rachel spent most of her remaining time during the war there. They worked six days per week, twelve hours per day for one week, and then one week of twelve hour nights, intermittently.

Rachel and the other girls performed hard work with liquid iron in front of extremely hot smelting ovens. They slept three or four kilometers away from the factory, on the floor, each with one blanket. It was winter time, and they had to walk to work. She had only one dress, socks and wooden shoes. When she walked with the other girls through the streets from the factory to where they slept, she looked in the windows and saw people sitting in their living rooms in light and warmth. She did not know what they did, and she could not remember having lived in a house or apartment or a place like these. The townspeople all saw the girls walking each day, turned their heads around so as not to see them, and did not do anything to help them.

While working as a slave worker, Rachel lost more weight because there was not enough food. Her breasts disappeared and she stopped menstruating. She said that the Germans put a chemical in their soup which made her and the others into sheep or zombies. Most of the workers were Jews and in the same situation that she was in. There were non-Jews who took care of the workers. Rachel recalled that one German man brought some food for them which he had to hide. If he were to have been caught, he would have been killed. The man did not have much money or food. His brother worked in a factory where they made margarine. He brought margarine for them in a piece of paper. For the rest of Rachel's life, she became extremely agitated and could never be around the smell of margarine again. Rachel ate only once a day, soup with a little piece of bread, and sometimes the margarine without anything else. Rachel recalled that not all of the people were bad, and some did try to do what they could to help.

In the winter of 1944-1945, the English bombed the area. When an alarm went off when the airplanes approached, everybody hid in the cellar in the factory or in cellars on the street, or in bomb shelters. The Jews were not allowed to use them. Jews had to wait on the street until everything was over. One time the airplanes were bombing the city, and one of Rachel's friends was in the street with her older sister. The older sister laid over Rachel's friend on the ground to protect her, and when the bombing stopped, Rachel's friend had to push her dead sister off of her. Rachel's friend was reunited with Rachel later in life in Israel, and she still cried over her sister and felt that it was her fault and that life was not worth living. Rachel's friend's brother, when he was freed, killed every German he could find, and died at an advanced age in Israel.

The factory was attacked regularly by bombers and many of the girls died. About 300 out of the 1200 girls survived the war. Rachel was not upset about the bombing as she believed that they were saviors who had come to liberate them. Throughout her life she remained upset that the Germans called it an attack.

In early April, 1945, the Germans told the girls that they had to leave the factory. They had to walk for several days. The Germans brought the girls, including Rachel, to a concentration camp called Bergen-Belsen, where they received no food and very little water. Rachel did not know how long she was there before the British rescued them. As the British army came closer and closer, individuals responsible for the camp ran away, leaving the prisoners without food or drink. The German soldiers knew that the war was going to end and that the British soldiers were coming, so they wanted to hide all of the dead persons before they left. There were thousands of dead bodies lying around as hundreds of people died there each day. All of the prisoners who could still walk had to bury the dead. There were huge holes where they put hundreds of dead bodies. Rachel, too, had to carry the dead to those graves. As the bodies had been dead for a long time, sometimes she would end up holding just an arm which came off when she tried to carry the body.

After the rescue, the surviving inmates continued to help place the dead in mass graves. An epidemic of typhus broke out and many more of the girls died. At the time of the rescue, Rachel weighed sixty pounds and barely knew her own name. When the British soldiers came, Rachel was lying on the floor. They thought she was dead. When they discovered that she was still alive, they took her to a nearby Sanatorium where German officers had been sent for recovery previously, and which had been changed into a hospital. English soldiers and doctors took care of her. When they took away Rachel's one dress, she was screaming and crying for it. She was naked under a clean blanket which was another humiliation for her. They controlled her eating which is why she survived. Others who walked away from the camp died after they were freed because they ate too much too quickly.

After the war, Rachel was the only female survivor of her family. Her mother, two sisters, many aunts and uncles, and her nieces and nephews were killed in Auschwitz. Some of the men in her family had been sent to work camps in Hungary and Romania, where they survived. Other sisters and brothers who had been living in the part of Romania that was not oc-cupied by the Germans had not been deported and sent to concentration camps and therefore survived. Of her family members who survived, some ended up in Israel, and others in South America, in Sao Paulo, Brazil. Of all of the Jews in Sighet, Rachel was one of only several hundred who survived.

Several months after Rachel was in the hospital, a rep-resentative from a Jewish agency went to Bergen-Belsen and brought Rachel back to Timisoara, Romania, where she spent the next few years. It is the part of Romania which had not been occupied, and where some of her siblings had survived. She lived with one of her surviving sisters. During that time, her relatives found food on a daily basis, mostly bread, under Rachel's pillows and under her bed. She experienced a break from reality during that time period and could not describe what she was feeling then, although she had been told that she was "not o.k. in her head."

In 1947, a man arrived in the town, who had survived the war in Palestine, and who had returned to look for his wife. He died soon afterwards. Rachel's nephew, who was about Rachel's age, assumed that man's passport and pretended to marry Rachel. They took off together on a ship to Palestine, as husband and wife, with the forged passport. The boat was intercepted off the coast of Palestine by the British authorities. They stayed there several days, anchored off the coast of Palestine, until a boat hired by one of Rachel's sisters, who had been living in Palestine, came to pick them up.

Upon her arrival in Palestine, it was discovered that Rachel was pregnant. When her family asked her who the father was, she was not clear, but said it might be the "nice, non-Jewish man who worked at the clothing factory where her sister worked." After her experiences, she took comfort in men who were nice to her. In 1948, she gave birth to a baby girl, Amos's sister. The baby was taken from her immediately upon her birth against Rachel's will. Her family had arranged for the baby to be adopted. Rachel had no memory of holding the baby. Although Rachel, throughout her life, and later with the help of Amos and his sister, made an attempt to locate her, they were unsuccessful in doing so. Rachel's family steadfastly refused to tell them where she was taken. Rachel could not bring herself to tell Amos about his sister until Amos was in his forties. To this day, Amos believes that some family members know where she is, but will not say. Rachel's entire family was Hasidic and she had been raised as an Orthodox Jew. The women were expected to marry young and to have children right away. Being unmarried, and having a baby out of wedlock, was viewed as a shame for the family, and so they wanted to hide the proof of her "sin."

Seven days after her child was born, Rachel joined the Israeli Army which was fighting against the Arabs. While in the army, she met Amos's father, Freddie, a romantic rebel, who was also a soldier in the Israeli Army. He worked as a messenger in the army, and rode on a Harley Davidson motorcycle. They met in a cafe. He had a dirt spot on his shirt from riding a motorcycle, and she helped him to clean it. That act was symbolic of their future relationship. Freddie was a concentration camp survivor as well, so they understood each other's traumas, but clearly it was Rachel who took care of Freddie. They married on January 16, 1949, shortly after the War of Independence in May of 1948. Three months after the wedding, Rachel became pregnant. Amos was born on January 27, 1950 in Haifa, Israel. After the wedding, they lived in Haifa in a converted garage in the back of a house with no running water or electricity. In order to have light at night, Freddie brought the motorbike into the garage and turned on its lights. Amos was born into a family situation with much love, but few resources.

Amos's father also had a profound influence on Amos. His story, before Amos was born, is described in the next Chapter.

# Chapter Two: Freddie

*"We're poor little lambs who've lost our way, Baa! Baa!*
*Baa! We're little black sheep who've gone astray, Baa-aa-aa!*
*Gentlemen-rankers out on the spree, Damned from here to*
*Eternity, God ha' mercy on such as we, Baa! Yah! Bah!"*

—Rudyard Kipling

Although they share certain traits, Amos has a different nature than his father Freddie had, and who is now deceased. Freddie was a survivor of Dachau, Buchenwald and Sachsenhausen Concentration Camps, and had severe post traumatic syndrome symptoms throughout his life as a result of his concentration camp experiences. He was unable to provide much financial support for the family, gambled most of the money away, and sometimes was unfaithful to Amos's mother. Despite all of the problems Freddie created in his family, some of which Amos was charged with setting right for his mother and sister's sake, Amos chose to remember his father's most positive qualities, of which there were many. He focused on his love for Amos, the times he did "come through" for him, his comedic nature, his ability to tell stories, his adventurous spirit, and his beautiful photography.

Amos saw his father clearly, but chose not to judge him. His father's ethics, borne out of his survivor experiences and his own predispositions, posed moral quandaries for Amos and for those who heard about his actions. Amos's compassion and love for his father are illustrative of his generous nature. Not all would be so forgiving. When Amos's father was about to die, he jokingly told Amos that he wanted to go to hell because none of his friends would be in heaven. Amos said if there was a heaven, his mother would be in it, as a saint, most likely, but agreed that nobody else Freddie loved to spend time with would be there.

Freddie was born on April 18, 1918 in Cologne, Germany, the youngest of four boys, in an assimilated German Jewish family. Freddie's father was a businessman. He owned a wholesale shoe store. His family came from the Frankfurt area. He had been a soldier in the German army of the Kaiser. Freddie's mother came from the west of Cologne. Both of their families had been in Germany for hundreds of years, and they thought of themselves as Germans first and Jews second. Freddie's mother died when he was only six years old, probably from tuberculosis. Freddie's father married his own cousin, who had been the nurse for Freddie's mother during her illness. Freddie told Amos that some believed that his step-mother had hastened his mother's death. Freddie was raised by his step-mother.

Freddie was handsome. He had a twinkle in his eyes, black curly hair, short stature, and a slight build. He was the black sheep of the family, and viewed himself as an outsider throughout his life. He had an artistic bent. He did not like playing by the rules, from an early age, and craved excitement, adventure, and the unconventional. He was a gambler. He liked people who misbehaved. He liked to misbehave. He liked gypsies and the downtrodden. He liked to talk with everyone, especially people who did not have any money or position in society. He liked to keep secrets. He was known to be a gifted raconteur. His stories were often embellished for dramatic effect, so it is impossible to know where the truth begins or ends in any of them. And, over time, he revealed different sides of the same stories to Amos. The content of these stories is revealing about his nature, whether they are entirely true or not, in that they show how he wished to be seen and how he viewed the world. We will never really know which stories are mostly facts, and which, embellished, but his time in concentration camps, and what occurred there, has been confirmed by others to Amos. One story goes that when he was twelve years old, Freddie went to the end of a train in Cologne, and while the driver went to lunch, Freddie took the train for a joy ride for a couple of hours. Amos claimed that family members confirmed that this event occurred.

Freddie was fourteen years old and in high school in Cologne when the Nazis took over in 1933. Freddie was upset that as a Jew he could not join the Hitler youth, because, in his limited world view at that time, they engaged in activities such as hiking, camping and games. Freddie excelled in sports and was a member of the Jewish sports group called the Maccabees. He was also a boxer, and, supposedly, was a German Maccabee boxing champion.

Freddie was expelled from gymnasium around age sixteen. There were different stories as to why he was expelled. No one really knows the reason for certain. He told Amos that around the time that Freddie was fifteen or sixteen years old, he had a German girlfriend whose father was a member of the Nazi party. Her father was upset that she was dating a Jewish boy, so he sent two men to talk to Freddie to "convince him" not to go out with her anymore. According to Freddie, he beat up both of them, and, because of this incident, he had to leave Germany for his own safety. He then worked on a transatlantic cruise ship between Bremerhaven, Germany and New York. Freddie learned how to cook on the ship. Amos's favorite dish, which Freddie made for him, was mashed potatoes and mache salad. Another dish Freddie made for him was "Hoppel Poppel," which is similar to "hash," and combines diced potatoes, onions, meat and eggs. While in New York, Freddie was usually docked in Hoboken, New Jersey, and he went through the Holland tunnel to get to New York City. After Amos moved to New York in the 1980's, he and his father retraced those steps by walking through the tunnel. Of course, it was (and still is) illegal to do so.

When Freddie was about sixteen or seventeen years of age, he worked on a different ship which transported heavy equipment between Germany and Spain. He ended up in Trieste, Italy, where he lived for about a year. Freddie was arrested by the Italian police in Trieste in 1936, and was handed over to the German police. He never told Amos why he was arrested. The German police transported Freddie to several different concentration camps, including Buchenwald, Sachsenhausen and Dachau.

While he was in Buchenwald, Freddie had to work in a stone quarry. He watched many prisoners being tortured and killed. While he was in Dachau, there was an event he told Amos about, which had a big impact on Amos's thinking about how to handle terrible situations. The prisoners, including Freddie, were forced to watch one prisoner being placed into a cement mixer. The mixer was turned on. Freddie told Amos that he heard his bones being broken and the prisoner screaming until he died. The prisoner standing next to Freddie started to shake and sob. Freddie told him to stop shaking and sobbing. The prisoner asked Freddie how this event could not affect him. Freddie told him to just think it is better him than you in the cement mixer. This philosophy allowed Freddie to endure the unimaginable, although it may not cast him in a sympathetic light. It is a survival technique pure and simple, with no time for sentiment or weakness. It is gratitude for not being the person the bad thing happened to.

Apparently someone photographed that event, and the photograph was published in foreign newspapers. When the photograph was published, the SS guards interrogated and tortured the prisoners to find out who took it. The prisoners were placed on forty-two days of solitary confinement. They received food once per day. The SS were never able to find out who did it. Freddie told Amos that it was one of the SS men who took the photograph and smuggled it out of the camp.

Freddie had a charismatic, engaging personality which served him well in concentration camp and throughout his life. One day, while in solitary confinement in Dachau, a group of SS men arrived from Berlin to inspect. The prisoners had to stand at attention, and Freddie was asked to introduce himself. He was supposed to say "swine Jew" and then his last name, which he did. Freddie then performed a backward somersault from a standing position in front of the visiting SS men, who were more amused by it than anything else. Another time, he developed a skin infection. Prisoners were usually killed if they had this. Freddie befriended the Nazi physician, and was treated without being killed.

Ironically, Freddie told Amos that it was while he was in Dachau that he had some of the most intellectually stimulating moments of his life which defined the rest of it. He was part of a group of inmates who were highly politically motivated, and it was there that Freddie received a political education. Among the inmates was Hans Litten, who was a famous lawyer, and about whom much has been written. Hans Litten was involved in bringing Hitler to court prior to 1933, and it was he who embarrassed Hitler with his scathing cross examinations. Because of this, Litten was continuously tortured in Dachau, which caused him to commit suicide, eventually, in February of 1938. Freddie and the other prisoners made sure he had the opportunity to do it, as an act of mercy, after they thought that he had lost his mind, in part, because he was building a crib for Christmas in 1937. Freddie always wanted Amos to become a lawyer because of having met Litten, and having been inspired by those who fought for justice as lawyers. It was Freddie who sent a letter to Hans Litten's mother to tell her what had happened to him, and Freddie's name is mentioned in books about Hans Litten.

For most of Amos's life, his father told him that he was released from Dachau early in 1939, but he never told Amos the circumstances of his release. It was only much later, in the mid 1990's, when Amos was living in New York, that Freddie finally told Amos what had happened. Freddie and Rachel visited Amos on a regular basis in New York City from the time Amos moved there in 1977. In the 1990's, Freddie and Rachel arrived late from the airport, and claimed, initially, that the plane had been delayed. The next day, Freddie took Amos aside and told him that when he arrived in customs at Kennedy airport, security there "found out about him" on the computers and what happened in Dachau. Freddie had a felony conviction and that is why American custom officials made it difficult for him to enter the United States. Freddie told Amos that while in Dachau, the SS officers had found him in bed one day with another younger boy, and accused him of being a homosexual. Freddie was sent to court in Munich, where a "show trial" took place to show the world how "badly" Jews behave. He was convicted of homosexuality and sent to prison for several months in Munich. The authorities at Kennedy airport found this conviction in the computer records they checked, although they had not been able to do so previously because the records had not been readily accessible prior to computers. There are court records which confirm this story.

Back in 1939, upon Freddie's release from prison, the prison authorities did not realize he came from a concentration camp, and they released him to the general public with the requirement that he leave Germany within forty-eight hours.

Freddie told Amos that while Freddie was in Dachau, his father and two of his brothers took all of the family's belongings, moved to Portugal, and then emigrated to Sao Paulo, Brazil, around 1938. Freddie felt abandoned by his father and those brothers. Freddie always told Amos that his father left with the two brothers, but Amos learned a few years ago, from letters which were found, that Freddie's father had remained in Germany and waited for Freddie to be released from Dachau before he left to join his two other sons. Freddie had asked them to send him money and they never did.

The second eldest brother had already emigrated to Palestine in the mid 1930's because of the Nazi takeover. After Freddie was released from prison, he left Germany and went to Palestine. While in Palestine, he took on several jobs, including gardening and selling ice cream and corn on the beach. He slept on roofs. During that time, he stole things. At one point he broke into a warehouse with carpets and stole them. He never felt apologetic about stealing things. He reasoned that after all that had happened to him, he did not have to abide by laws. If he needed money for food and shelter, he would have to take what he could to survive. He also started to write an account of his time in the concentration camps. He went to the offices of a newspaper, and tried to publish his accounts. One day, the British Intelligence Service called Freddie in and accused him of being a spy for the Germans. They stated that nobody but a German spy would know about what happened in concentration camps and no one was ever released alive from them. According to Freddie, the British Intelligence Service took away his writings and threatened him with punishment if he ever published those accounts.

In 1942, Freddie joined the British Army and became part of the Jewish Battalion. He was stationed in Northern Africa, in Egypt, during the battle of El Alamein, due west of Alexandria, and charged with interrogating German prisoners of war. This was the location where a decisive battle had occurred and the British defeated the Germans. At the end of the war, in 1945, Freddie returned to Palestine. He had written many letters to his father, who was in Brazil, telling him how miserable he was in Israel, and asking him for help to move to Brazil. Freddie eventually received a letter back from his two brothers, who told him to stop bothering their father. They admitted that they had not given the letters he had sent to their father because they were "too rude and desperate," and they did not want their father to be hurt. They also said that they could not send him a ticket to Brazil because they had no money, and that all of the money was invested in a textile factory in Brazil.

Freddie's father died in 1947, and his property was taken over by the two brothers. Freddie never received any monies from his father's estate or from his father's business. For the rest of his life, there was a terrible tension between Freddie and the two brothers as their father's factory eventually expanded and the two brothers became multi-billionaires. Their children now run that factory. Freddie struggled to survive financially and was never helped by his family of origin. Years later, Amos and his sister hired lawyers in Brazil to see if they could reclaim the estate. The lawyers told them it would be futile to pursue it at that point.

Realizing that moving to Brazil would not be a viable option, Freddie then joined the Jewish underground in Palestine, the Haganah, to fight the British. There were several underground groups, and Freddie joined the one that was most left wing and liberal. He was part of the German Jewish emigrant group of people raised in Germany who were teenagers and in their early twenties during that time in Palestine. Freddie was involved in many battles in Tel Aviv and Haifa, and in rescuing Jerusalem. He was homeless for much of the time that he was part of the Haganah, and he was sick from malaria. Then, shortly before Israel was declared a State in May of 1948, Freddie joined the official Israeli Army. When Israel was created, the Haganah had merged into the Israeli Army.

At some point in April of 1948, a good friend of Freddie's asked him to join him to "pay back" the Arabs during the Civil War. Freddie refused. The next day, his friend came back with both arms drenched in blood. Freddie later learned that the blood was from the massacre which had occurred in Deir Yassin, where over one hundred villagers were killed outside of Jerusalem. A group of fighters from paramilitary groups, including Freddie's friend, had massacred villagers, including women and children. It was at that point that Freddie realized that the conflict between the Jews and the Arabs might never end, and he decided that he would eventually make plans to leave Israel permanently. It was at the end of the war between the Arabs and Jews, in the end of 1948, that Freddie met Rachel.

Amos's early life with his parents, in Amos's mind, was relatively unscathed by his parents' difficult experiences. The next Chapter deals with that time period.

# Chapter Three: Amos's Early Years: Birth to Age Ten

*"When you're hungry, sing; when you're hurt, laugh"*
—Jewish Proverb

*"We don't see things the way they are.*
*We see them the way we are"*

—Talmud

Amos was born on January 27, 1950 in Haifa, Israel. Ironically, that was the same date that Auschwitz had been liberated five years earlier. His parents were living in poverty, each having lost their own parents and most of their respective families, but they were determined to make their newly created family strong. When Amos was a baby, he contracted pneumonia. The pediatrician told his parents that he needed antibiotics, which at that time were minimally available in Israel as they had just been developed. Amos's parents were also told that antibiotics were not available for civilians, but were given only to military doctors for soldiers. Amos's father, Freddie, went to the Chief Medical Officer of the Israeli Army and asked him for some antibiotics for Amos. Freddie was told again that the antibiotics were only for Israeli soldiers, not for civilians. As the story goes, Freddie pulled out a gun and told the medic that he fought for Israel and that his son deserved to be taken care of. The medic gave the antibiotic to him and did not report him to the authorities. Amos cherished that story because his father's love for him was so apparent in it, and it cast Freddie as a strong and able protector and hero. Amos recovered, thrived, and learned to speak Hebrew. Photographs of Amos during that period show a happy, healthy baby and toddler.

When Amos was three years old, in 1953, the family moved to Cologne, Germany via a boat to France. Freddie always felt that Israel was a temporary place to live and told Amos's mother, Rachel, from the time he met her, that he wanted to move back to Germany since Brazil was not an option. Freddie saw himself as German, and did not want to be around the fighting in Israel. In addition, Freddie had contracted malaria in Palestine, which made him sicker in warm climates, and there was no real treatment for it. When the family arrived in Germany, one of Freddie's brothers, with whom he was close, had already moved to Cologne from Palestine. He was their only family member there. Over ninety percent of Cologne had been destroyed in the war. Thus, there was a shortage of housing as most of it had been completely eliminated.

Initially, Amos lived with his parents in a building close to the Rhine river. It was one of the few buildings which had not been bombed out, and had consisted of fancy apartments before the war. Each room was divided into two or three rooms by thin walls. Multiple families lived in the same room, separated by those walls. His mother worked in a chocolate factory where she made macaroons. She brought some home at night to feed the family, which at times were their only meal for dinner. The macaroons were organized on a conveyor belt, exactly as the chocolates appeared in the famous scene in the television show "I love Lucy." Amos's father was sick, initially, from malaria, and could not work at all. Later, he was able to work as a photographer. He was self-taught and had started to do photography in Israel. Cologne was known for its trade shows, and Freddie worked at them. He also went to public events, as well as to bars and pubs, to take photographs. He was paid by the people whose photographs he took.

Amos attended a Catholic kindergarten run by nuns, initially. It was part of the church. Amos spoke only Hebrew when he first arrived in Germany. He learned German within three months of arriving there, and "unlearned" Hebrew for the rest of his life. Amos recalled that the nuns hit him with rulers when teaching him to learn German. However, later on, when he was six or seven years old, as he described it, some remnants of Hebrew came out in his German. He was lisping. Amos had to go for speech therapy for two years. He recalled that people made fun of him until he was about ten or eleven for his lisping. Although Amos did not like being teased, he was not a person to take it too much to heart. It is that quality in his personality which always saved him from a lot of heartache.

In the neighborhood, there was a small street next to the house where Amos lived. There were women standing on the street on a regular basis. A brothel was located in the middle of the street. Cologne was known to have several of those streets in those years. When Amos was about four years old, he asked his mother for an explanation as to why the women were there. Although they were prostitutes, Rachel told Amos that they did not have husbands, and that they were each looking for one. This was one of the first examples Amos remembers of his mother trying to protect him by telling him a story. His father took photographs of the prostitutes and pimps, and was always friendly with everyone, no matter their station in society. Amos inherited this ability to relate to people on all different levels, and to find common ground.

When Amos was about five years old, Amos and his family moved across the Rhine River to another neighborhood outside the center of Cologne. It was an industrial neighborhood which consisted of new buildings. They moved to a one bedroom apartment in one of the new buildings, and stayed there until 1963. There was a pharmacy on the ground floor, a doctor in the building, and a pub across the street. Half of the buildings in the area were pre-war, and were in the process of being renovated, and the other half were new. The neighborhood was dominated by the chemical factory which was close by. Amos remembered that the air was yellow and smelled on a regular basis. Amos attended a kindergarten in the Protestant Church around the corner from his apartment. The schools were either Catholic or Protestant. Amos's sister was born in 1955, a year before Amos entered elementary school.

Amos started to attend elementary school when he was six years of age. He attended the school through age ten, as was customary, and he had one teacher throughout that time. He did not want to go to the Catholic elementary school which was closer by, but attended the Protestant public school instead. He did not want to be near the nuns because of what had occurred earlier. There was a bunker across from the elementary school which was thick with concrete walls, a visible and constant reminder of what was.

Amos recalled that he was the teacher's pet. She favored him, and saw something special about him, which gave him confidence. Amos enjoyed school, had many good friends, and liked performing arts. His best friend when he was eight or nine was a girl. Amos only learned later in life that this best friend was Jewish, as her parents did not tell her until she was much older. Her parents had been imprisoned in concentration camps, but tried to hide that they were Jewish out of fear. Amos's parents never hid their backgrounds.

Amos's sister was impacted by their parent's history in a way which differed from Amos's experience. She stopped eating when she was about four years old and was sent to the hospital. Because Rachel had nearly starved, it was very important to her that her children had good food, especially breakfast. She continually insisted that they eat, as in her world view, that might be their last meal for a while. Amos's sister rebelled because she did not want pressure to eat, and she wanted to differentiate herself from her mother's issues regarding food. Their parents insisted on good behavior after all they had been through in their life. Throughout her early life, Amos's sister fought against her parents and often did not do what they or anyone else expected. She felt guilty about that.

Amos, on the other hand, did not fight with his parents and was obedient. He wanted to save them from any additional pain and was extremely protective of them. As the son, he had a special status in the family. He was intelligent, friendly and good looking in a Dutch way. His sister was always fighting with everyone, she had dark, kinky hair and looked like a gypsy, and was not as generally accepted, although Amos was always kind and loving towards her. Amos was the hope of the family. He wanted to prove to his parents that their lives were worth living after all they had been through. His sister wanted to prove that she was different from them, and that she was not going to be controlled by their post traumatic reactions to things.

When Amos was young, his father often remained in bed for days and days. Whenever his children needed him, Freddie woke up right away and was friendly and helped. He slept to escape. When he was not sleeping, he often stayed in bed, where he smoked cigarettes, read the newspaper, and ate meals. Freddie often stayed in the bath for hours, also, where he read the newspaper. Amos never saw this as different or as a problem. Amos saw his father as someone who had a huge zest for life, and not as being a depressive type. An example of his zest was when Freddie would take the neighborhood children around the block in his car, which was the newest car in the neighborhood.

Amos did not realize that his father suffered from post traumatic stress syndrome, or that such a syndrome was associated with concentration camp victims. His father was always reading the newspaper, as he wanted to stay on top of events so if they had to flee, or do something different, he would know right away and be prepared for himself and the family. Freddie taught Amos that he should not look at himself as Jewish, but as a German, and that he should try to fit in with the other Germans. He also taught Amos that Amos should not look at himself as smarter than the others.

Freddie thought of himself as a Communist first, in the sense that he believed that society must take care of the down-trodden. Freddie also thought of himself as German, and being a German to him meant German history and the German culture of Schiller and Goethe. Freddie did not identify with being Jewish, and taught Amos that he should not consider himself different because he was Jewish. He taught Amos that it is just one of many religions, and that Amos should be integrated and assimilated.

Amos's mother still had many of the remnants of her Hasidic background, including her devotion to family, her attempt to keep a Jewish home, and her modest dress. Amos's mother took responsibility for the children, the cooking, and caring for the home. She was always there for the family and always functioning. Amos maintained that she was consistently in a good mood. When Amos learned to write at age six, his mother learned to write in German with him, and they had similar handwriting because of that. Sometimes she would do Amos's homework, which he thought of as an example of a mother's love.

It was difficult for his mother to help Amos and his sister outside of the home. Rachel and Freddie were afraid of German adults, and Rachel was not comfortable speaking German, so if there were any issues at school, they could not handle it. It became Amos's responsibility to take care of his sister. As early as the age of ten, Amos would go to the school and speak with the professionals if there were problems with his sister and her behavior, or for any other issue. Amos oftentimes served as the interpreter between his family and the outside world. Amos, in effect, ran the family from an early age, and they all depended on him for his strength, intelligence and competence.

There were always visitors in their apartment. His parents had an active social life, and the neighbors and many other people loved them. Amos described them as being gentle, nice and open people. His mother was constantly cooking for everyone, and readily took people into their home. Freddie's friend from London, England, whom Freddie met in Israel, his wife, and two children, went to Germany several times a year, and lived with Amos's family in their one bedroom apartment for about four weeks. They put mattresses on the floor. The parents all slept in the living room, and the children all slept in the children's room. Many other people stayed with Amos's family too. At one point, Amos recalled that his mother's sister came from Romania on her way to Israel with her twin sons, and lived with them over an extended period. Throughout that time period, Amos did not realize that he had relatives in Israel.

Amos recalled that his world became broader than Germany at an early age. He had extended family throughout the world, he and his immediate family did a lot of traveling, and Amos was a voracious newspaper reader. One time, an Aunt from his father's side of the family, who lived in Brooklyn on Eastern Parkway, sent him a care package which consisted of a Davy Crockett hat, along with a cowboy gun belt and fake gun. Amos said that this gift was memorable because it exposed him to another culture, and kindled a lifelong love of family, New York and of travel. Amos was aware, at that time, that other Jews had emigrated to the United States. He and his family admired the United States as they credited the United States with the rescue of the Jews from the Nazis.

From an early age, Amos and his father went to London, England on an annual basis to visit his father's German friend whom he met when he lived in Israel, and who was a committed Communist. They would all go to the Aldermaston March, the annual Easter March, which was the largest protest march for peace. The peace sign originated from that event. Amos was exposed to anti-nuclear war activists, anarchists, and to the music of Joan Baez, Donovan and others. This was Amos's first memory of attending a protest march. Amos later learned that his parents were the only individuals in their community who voted for Communists during the elections in Cologne.

Amos's father made certain that Amos had many, diverse and interesting experiences at an early age. Amos went with his father to the boat races between Oxford and Cambridge Universities which took place on the Thames River. Amos also took a trip to Paris with his father. Amos recalled that one of the days was extremely hot. Amos's father bet him that he would not jump into the Seine River. Amos, who was not one to lose a bet, slipped into the water from the riverbank. This was an example of the lifelong banter between father and son, and their mutual love of adventure and amusement.

During the summers, and during Easter vacation time, Amos's family sometimes went to Belgium and stayed at a bed and breakfast by the water. Amos remembered those times as idyllic. He recalled one time, however, when he went to the local playground there with his mother and sister. When people on the playground asked his mother where she was from, she said Germany. The people told her that they did not like the Germans as they "flooded" their Country and brought havoc to it. They made her leave the playground with Amos and his sister. Rachel did not tell them that she was Jewish and was in a Concentration Camp. Rachel later cried about it to Freddie. This incident made a deep impression on Amos.

During some of the summers during this period, Amos and his family drove over the Alps to Opatija, which was a coastal town on the Adriatic Sea, in what was then Yugoslavia, and what is now Croatia, and vacationed there. The cost of living there was much cheaper than in Germany, and Amos and his family, despite their small budget, thoroughly enjoyed their time there. Amos also recalled spending time in Venice, Italy, and in other locations in Italy with his family. Although Amos's family was of limited means, they lived life large, and they did not let their finances prevent them from visiting different countries.

Amos and his family also visited his mother's Hasidic family in Antwerp, Belgium during the Jewish holidays. One family member, a boy who was Amos's age, had cerebral palsy.

Amos remembered that the boy was extremely intelligent. At the time, Amos could not understand how even though the boy's brain could work so well, he had no control over his movements. The boy's condition sparked Amos's curiosity and his wanting to learn more. It was only later, with medical training, that Amos fully understood the condition.

On one occasion on the way home from Antwerp, Amos's family drove through Brussels, Belgium. As they walked through the streets, Amos's mother started screaming, and quickly crossed the street. She had recognized one of her Uncles from her mother's family, whom she thought had been killed in the war. He would not hug or touch her, as was the Hasidic custom. Amos's mother felt bereft because of a custom which she felt had no meaning in their circumstance. She had become so removed from that life. It seemed wrong to Amos's mother that two survivors of unimaginable horror from the same family could not show each other affection.

Amos went to local fairs with his family a couple of times a year. They had small rides and games. Amos was completely enamored with a game of chance, and he liked to gamble a bit. Amos's father, however, had a serious issue with gambling. From the time Amos was about eight or nine years old, Amos had to go by bus and train to the center of Cologne to look for his father, who liked to stay overnight in illegal gambling joints. Amos's mother would send Amos to find his father, as she did not feel comfortable doing so. This would occur several times per month. His mother would stay with his sister. His father would go from one gambling joint to another, and his mother would ask Amos to find out the addresses for these locations. When Amos finally found him each time, Amos would tell him that "Mom wants you home." Amos had to walk into these places alone to find him. Freddie would then go home, but often after he had spent all of the money that the family needed. Sometimes he would disappear for days.

From the time Amos could remember, in addition to having a lot of responsibility for his family, he had a lot of freedom. He could play outside with his many friends as much as he wanted to. He was part of a group of boys that liked to play a game as knights. They made swords out of wooden sticks and fought each other. They made the armor out of boxes.

Amos's recollections from those years were mostly positive. He remembered one traumatic incident from when he was about eight years old. Amos was invited to a boy's birthday party, who was then his best friend. He was not Jewish. The boy's family and his and Amos's other friends were there. After the main dish was served, and before the dessert, Amos asked where the bathroom was located. Amos went to the bathroom. When he returned to the party, his friend did not talk to him as much as before. The next day, his friend told him that his parents said he could not play with him anymore because they said it was very rude to get up and go to the bathroom in the middle of a meal. His friend never played with him again. About six months later, his friend then left school and moved away. Shortly after he moved, Amos's family read in the newspaper that his friend's father came home drunk one day, killed the whole family, and then killed himself.

At about the same age, Amos suffered more trauma. He would regularly go to the local quarry, which was filled with water. Amos and his friends went swimming there as a group. They had to walk twenty minutes in the woods to get to the quarry. The waters were treacherous and deep and the temperature of the water changed from one area to the other. There was no adult supervision. After one of Amos's friends drowned there, Amos was determined to become a good swimmer so that the same thing would not happen to him. (In his early teens, Amos became a champion swimmer for the Cologne swim team. He had attended the Cologne swim club for many years. When he reached puberty, he realized that he did not grow as fast as the others and that height, at least for short distances, was important. Thus, he did not further pursue swimming professionally).

Amos's sights were set high from the outset. He was always looking to better his situation and that of his family. As bad a businessman as Freddie was, that was how good Amos was. He was his own lucky penny. Because of Freddie's difficulties working, and his constant gambling, Amos became an entrepreneur at a very early age, which was not something he had learned in the German culture at that time. When he was age eight he played with marbles, which were valuable. Amos took a shoe box, inverted it, and cut out small holes. There were different size holes in a row. He numbered the holes. Amos put the shoe box against the wall. He told the children in the neighborhood to roll the marble, and if it went through one of the holes, Amos would multiply their marbles by the number on the hole. If the marble did not go through the hole, Amos would keep the marble. Amos staged it so that he could keep everybody's marbles. One day the father of one of the children told Amos's father that his son had lost all of his marbles to Amos, and that Amos should give him his marbles back. Amos's father made him give the marbles back.

No task was too much for Amos when it came to making money. At around the same time, Amos worked at a gas station on the weekends. He would clean windshields for tips. Amos also did work for the pub across the street. He would take kegs they filled up with beer, and take them from the pub to people's homes, as there was no beer in bottles at the time. On the weekends, on occasion, he went with his father to industrial exhibits where his father took photographs, either in the City of Cologne or in the City of Dusseldorf. A famous symbol of Dusseldorf was a cartwheeler. Amos did cartwheels in front of the exhibit halls, and received tips for that. He remembered the thrill of performing in front of a crowd, and of being paid for it.

Amos's recollection is that during his early years, his parents did not talk about the Holocaust. They wanted him to become integrated into German society as much as possible. It was important to his parents that he become a "good German" and that he not be different from the rest of the neighbors. This is curious as his father was the black sheep of his family and a lifelong rebel, and his mother rebelled from her Hasidic roots. Amos recalled that his parents taught him the values of hard work, punctuality, cleanliness, and the importance of being well dressed and groomed. They wanted him to understand how the world worked politically. Amos started to read the entire newspaper starting at age six or seven. He read a political magazine called Der Spiegel each week. His parents were never able to save any money, and they lived from one month to the next, mostly from the earnings of his father as a photographer and from German reparation money. The reparation money was called "Wiedergutmachung," which roughly translates into English as "making good again." Amos began to fill the financial gaps with his entrepreneurial activities.

In Germany, at that time, reparation monies were dependent upon the percentage of disability each person was assessed at. On a regular basis, recipients of reparation monies had to be re-examined to reassess their percentage of disability. Amos's mother was assessed initially as thirty to forty percent disabled, whereas his father was assessed at fifty to sixty percent disabled. The higher the percentage of disability, the more money the person would receive. Amos's father determined that in order to get more money, he needed to have a higher disability percentage. In order to achieve that, he regularly saw physicians and psychiatrists who had assessed, in the early 1960's, that his condition had worsened. Whether it had or not is uncertain, as the story below will illustrate. At one point, Freddie was admitted to an inpatient psychiatric unit to be evaluated. When Amos and his mother visited Freddie while he was there, Freddie walked over to them very slowly, with his eyes down, in what looked to be a catatonic-like state. As Freddie drew closer to Amos and his mother, he looked up at them, looked around to make certain no one was watching, and then winked his eye at them and smiled. Freddie was reassessed as ninety percent disabled. Many years later, Amos was reminded of that incident when he watched the movie "One Flew Over the Cuckoo's Nest," starring Jack Nicholson. It was as if the character played by Nicholson, Randle Patrick McMurphy, had learned from Freddie's play book. Amos, in looking back, truly believed that his father was unable to hold down a regular job due to his post traumatic stress, he had inadequate formal education, and that whatever the percentage assessed, his father was severely damaged by his wartime experiences. In addition, he recognized that his father knew how to work the system, and that after what had happened to him, Freddie would not play by the rules. Freddie maintained that he would not have survived if he had played by the rules. In addition, Freddie thought that he was owed a lot. This attitude has caused much confusion for Amos in terms of what were the correct ethics, and yet, his deep love for his father was what stood out most prominently in his thinking.

When Amos was a child, his parents would instruct him to run into a field where corn was grown to grab some for the family. His parents would serve as the "lookouts." There was no corn available in the stores at that time. On some level, Amos realized even then that his ethics were being compromised, but his family came first, and that is what they asked of him.

Amos and his family did not have stability in their housing situation. Due to Amos's father's inability to work regularly, and his gambling away what money they did have, they were dispossessed from their home many times when Amos was between the ages of six and ten years old. Amos recalled that people came and put stickers on their furniture one of the times. The stickers had a German eagle on it. It was illegal to remove the sticker. By putting a stamp on the furniture, it meant that the furniture did not belong to you anymore. Amos thought of being dispossessed as part of normal life. It was all he knew. Although it must have been embarrassing for his mother, in particular, she did not show it. At one point, Amos's father pawned off his own wedding ring, and that of Amos's mother. He did not see his mother cry about it. When Freddie had money, he would sometimes go to pawning auctions and buy items there. Possessions came and went. Amos learned not to hold onto "things" too tightly, although his penchant for collecting objects in his adult years is probably linked in some way to those early deprivations and losses.

Nothing seemed to phase Amos much even in the early years, or at least he would not admit it to himself. There were no Jews in the neighborhood where he lived and no Jews in his grade school, to his knowledge. Despite this, Amos did not remember ever feeling alienated or that he did not belong. Everybody knew he was Jewish, but nobody talked about the war, and if they did, they all said they did not know what happened to the Jews. The Germans he interacted with professed that they were not certain that the concentration camps really existed. Amos's father did not have ill feelings against the Germans. Freddie believed that there was inherent good in all people and that no one was ever born "bad." He believed that the government can make people into bad people. There was never any finger pointing in Amos's family. At no point did Amos hear accusatory words from his mother or father against the Germans or their neighbors. His parents taught him to be a good person and to help those in need. Throughout all of his parent's terrible war time experiences, sometimes Jews helped them, and sometimes non-Jews did. Their lines of who was good and who was bad were not drawn by religion, or by any other partisan stereotype. Amos's mother, however, never felt quite at home in Germany, and always "slept with one eye open." Amos did not know this until many years later when his mother told him this after she moved to Israel and after his father died.

When Amos was nine years old, it was time to decide if he would attend a more advanced school, or if he would remain where he was until age fourteen. The vast majority of the children stayed. At that time, less than one in ten children moved from elementary school to gymnasium. Amos was determined to go to gymnasium so that he could attend University. Children attended gymnasium from ages ten to nineteen. Amos's father had attended gymnasium until he was expelled at around age sixteen. Amos's father wanted him to go to the natural sciences gymnasium from which he had been expelled. Someone living in their building suggested that Amos should look at another more humanistic gymnasium closer to where they lived. In order to be accepted, Amos had to be tested. It was his first big test. The test consisted of applicants being asked questions in a school classroom at that humanistic gymnasium. The teacher asked the class to explain how a fish hook worked. When Amos went to Belgium with his family, he would fish. Amos was able to draw a fish hook and to explain how it worked in great detail. He was thereafter accepted into gymnasium, the first of many future achievements.

# Chapter Four:
# Amos's Gymnasium Years:
# Ages Ten to Eighteen

*"Money lost, nothing lost. Courage lost, everything lost"*
—Yiddish Proverb

*"Don't be sweet, lest you be eaten up;*
*don't be bitter lest you be spewed out"*
—Jewish Proverb

Amos's education, both in the world, and in the classroom, further enlivened his curiosity and passions. He continued to vacation with his family in Belgium, Yugoslavia, and Italy. He continued to attend the anti-nuclear war Easter peace marches in England on a yearly basis with his father. These were defining moments because Amos realized that other countries had a lot to offer, and there was a world he wanted to further explore beyond Germany.

Because of his mother's influence, he began to attend synagogue in Cologne on a regular basis. The synagogue had re-opened in 1959. There was a day care and youth groups at the synagogue. Amos played basketball there. He recalled that he felt safe at the Temple because he was exposed, finally, to people who were more similar to him in intellect, thinking and background. Most of the children had parents who were concentration camp survivors. The children played predominantly at Amos's home rather than his going to their homes. Amos recognized that these parents were damaged, perhaps more than his parents. Many of the other parents were cautious, they did not invite people to their houses, they were not intellectual, and many were not German. They came from Eastern Europe, many were Polish, while some were from Hungary or Austria. They spoke German with an accent. Some tried to eat Kosher food, but there was no truly Kosher store in Cologne at that time. A few times a year, a man came from Antwerp, which had a large Jewish religious community, and sold Kosher meats in the synagogue, which were more costly, so not everyone could afford to buy them.

Amos attended, also, a Jewish youth camp named Sobernheim a few hours from Cologne, in both the summer and winter, until age sixteen. Jews from all over Germany attended the camp. They ate Kosher food, and were immersed in the Jewish religion and in what it meant to be a Jew culturally. Many times Amos's family did not have enough money to pay for the camp. Amos's father would perform a special job to make money specifically to pay for it.

Amos recalled that during those years, he had significant constipation when he lived in Cologne. When he was at the Jewish youth camp, it was the only time he had regular stools. This physical manifestation is significant because it shows that although his mind was able to bury certain discomforts, his body would not let him. He admitted that he was happier at the Jewish youth camp because he met other children who were intelligent, who liked to talk, who were good looking, and who liked to play. Being Jewish was not an issue at the camp. Since Amos, from the age of three, had always lived around Christian Germans, being Jewish was an issue, whether he was aware of it or not. It was an issue because he knew, at some point, and the other families knew, that his parents were different, that his mother did not come from Germany, and that his parents had been in concentration camps. When Amos was younger, the differences did not quite resonate with him. Starting around age ten, he became more acutely aware that less than twenty years before, the Nazis ruled Germany. Amos was reminded of the war every single day when he walked past destroyed and bombed out buildings which littered the entire City of Cologne. He did not discuss the war with his German friends. Amos did not recall that he discussed the war with his Jewish camp friends.

Amos's family's home continued to be open. They had many international friends. Amos's father had a friend born in India, and his friend's brother, who both lived in England and travelled to Germany several times a year to visit them. They were manual laborers who had never married. These friends would live with them, and, on occasion, cook Indian food for Amos's family. Amos learned about Bolst's curry powder, and years later, he was pleased to find it being sold in Manhattan in Curry Hill on Lexington Avenue.

With regard to his school education, Amos was chosen to be one of the students at the all boys gymnasium after he passed the interview. Amos understood that nobody in his immediate family had attended University, and that this was the first step on the path to it. At that point, he had no idea what he would want to study at University. His parents made it clear to him on a continuous basis that studying at gymnasium was what he needed to be doing at that time.

Neither of Amos's parents wanted him to go into business. Amos's father, especially, wanted him to become a professional. His father had fond memories of people whom he met in Dachau, especially Hans Litten, who had been the top lawyer in Germany in the early 1930's when Hitler was brought to Court, and was intensely questioned by Litten. As soon as Hitler took over Germany, Hans Litten had been arrested and brought to several different concentration camps, including Dachau, where, in 1937, Amos's father first met him. Amos's father wanted Amos to become a lawyer to advocate for the underclasses.

When Amos was age ten, his father wrote him a thoughtful letter, which Amos has always kept. His father reminded him to take care of the poor people in the world and not to forget them, or to put blinders on, no matter how successful Amos might become. He told Amos to use every opportunity to learn a lot so that others would not think of him as ignorant. He told Amos that once he became strong, he must teach those who are poor his knowledge, so that all people in the world, including Amos, would have true happiness and contentment. His father told him that it was probably too early for him to remember these lessons, but that he should keep the letter in a safe place so that he could read it and understand it later. He told Amos that he wanted him to be happy and content. Amos opined that some other parents probably wanted their children to become financially successful, but his father, from early on, reminded him that service to others, and happiness and contentment, were of paramount importance.

Amos's father often told him that when he was in Dachau, he met the smartest people in Germany, who were all assembled in one place at that time. He wanted Amos to learn from them and to become a better person. Amos's mother emphasized that she came from a Jewish family, and she wanted to bring some religion into Amos's life, but since there were no Jews in the neighborhood, that occurred when he started synagogue. That was the informal education he received at home and in his Jewish community.

In the secular world, from the time Amos began gymnasium at age ten, he travelled by himself by bus, and then by train, to get to school. On the first day, Amos went to school by himself. He missed the exit for the train, and had to walk over the Rhine Bridge. He found his way to school. Amos had no idea why his parents did not take him that first day. On an existential level, Amos felt that he was by himself all of the time, and that he had to take care of himself. On that day, he remembered an incident which occurred when he was age eight. The family was returning home from Cologne by car, he fought with his parents, he remembered that he was not behaving, and he asked to be let out of the car. He never expected that his parents would do so. In the middle of the bridge in Cologne, his father stopped the car and let him out. He was about two miles from the house which was a forty-five minute walk. He found his way home. By remembering that incident, it gave him confidence that he would find the school too.

When Amos was in his elementary school years, he recalled that, in his view, the other parents were not intellectually sophisticated. He described them as more blue collar in background. In his gymnasium years, he was exposed to wealthier, more educated families. The students' fathers had steady employment and they had grandparents and larger families. They lived in green, leafy neighborhoods. They had houses with large kitchens, and impressive stoves, and bigger cars. By contrast, Amos never had grandparents or much family as they had all been killed in the war. Amos and his family lived in a neighborhood with tiny apartments without central heating and without warm water. They took only one bath per week. Amos had to bring up coal from the basement once per week in order to heat up the bath water. There was only enough water for one full bath. First he and his sister took a bath, and then his parents took their turn. As the water became colder, his mother went to the stove to heat up more hot water to pour into the bathtub. Amos ate German food the way the other families did in his neighborhood. For breakfast, he had cold cuts, fresh rolls from the bakery, eggs, tomatoes and cucumbers. He brought a sandwich to school for lunch. For dinner, his mother cooked either German or Hungarian/ Austrian food. He typically ate schnitzel, goulash, chicken, potatoes, and pasta with cocoa and sugar. Amos recognized that there was a difference between how he lived, and how many of the students lived whom he met at the gymnasium, but he did not ascribe a value to it.

When Amos was thirteen years old, he and his family moved from that poor neighborhood to the suburbs, to a town called Bensberg. It was a new development. His parents received money from the government, and that is how they were able to pay for it. Amos felt that living in a better neighborhood and house made a big difference for him. There were even more people visiting and staying over, and his life had more permanency and stability. His Jewish friends came to visit from Cologne. On Jewish holidays, several of his Jewish friends took a tram from synagogue, a forty minute ride, to his parent's home.

Amos continued to be in charge of many of the major decisions of the family, including education and finances. When Amos was eleven years old, he chose which elementary school his sister attended. When there were questions about money, Amos was always involved. Amos decided how the money was spent, starting when he was around age ten. His parents ceded these decisions over to him. They felt that he was smarter than they were and that he was able to balance things and to make better decisions. It was Amos who made such determinations as what furniture to buy, what clothing to purchase, what to plant in the garden and where to go for vacation. He continued to attend the parent-teacher conferences for his sister with his parents. He remained the one to get his father out of the gambling joints and back home.

Amos became more worldly by virtue of his command of languages. Starting at age ten, he learned Latin for eight years. He maintained that Latin influenced him the most as it gave him a universal way to look at languages. He believed that everyone should still be required to take it. At the age of twelve, he was required to choose to learn French or English, and then one year later, he was required to take the other language. Amos chose French and then English, as he did not consider that he would live in an English speaking country at that time.

During the gymnasium years, Amos did not do well in school. He was in the lower third of his class. A couple of years he nearly failed. He was among the youngest in his class. He did not know how to learn, he did not spend much time reading, and he invested little time in his homework. His emphasis was on playing with his friends and working to make money for the family. Amos's parents did get him tutors in the subjects that he did not do well in, but they did not put pressure on him to get good grades.

When Amos was age thirteen, he found an opportunity, which was another life-changing event. He was an exchange student through a program at the synagogue. He spent three weeks with a French boy and his family. They were Jewish, the father was a banker, and they were financially in the upper class. Amos observed firsthand the lifestyle of wealthy Jews, which did not exist in Cologne. The apartments and houses Amos saw were bigger than anything he had experienced before, the furniture and decor was more elaborate, the food more elegant and their clothing was expensive and stylish.

He first lived in Paris, and then went to the South of France, to Arcachon, with the French family. This exposure to another culture made him realize that he wanted to keep experiencing more than just his life in Germany. He remembered that the food in France was fresher and cooked better. He was exposed to French music. He saw Jacques Brel perform live. He learned to speak French more fluently, and read a French newspaper. When he travelled with the French family to the South of France, he went to a vineyard, ate seafood, and ate lobster for the first time at a location halfway from Paris to Arcachon. When they went to an oyster farm, Amos tried to take one, and he cut his pinky in half when he tried to remove it.

Even though Amos was getting a taste of the "good life," he recalled that he did not feel comfortable with that family, because he imagined that they looked down on him because he did not come from the same social class. He did not have their sophistication and manners. He watched how they behaved, but was not always able to match his behavior with theirs. Nonetheless, he was grateful for the opportunity and for the exposure to that culture. Around the time of that visit, in 1963, Amos recalled that the Vietnam War had erupted, and that President Kennedy was killed. He remembered that attitudes changed around the world, including Germany, during the Vietnam War years. These were important years in Amos's development, and in the history of the world.

When Amos was age thirteen, he had another pivotal event, his Bar Mitzvah. Amos was among the first post-war Jewish boys who had a Bar Mitzvah in the new synagogue in Cologne. In order to have the Bar Mitzvah, he had to study with the Cantor once per week for about a year to learn his portion of the Torah. The lessons took place in the private apartment of the Cantor in the synagogue. Amos recalled that the Cantor would sit too close to him, and several times put his hand on Amos's upper leg. Amos thought that it was odd, but did not think much of it at the time. Amos pulled his leg away each time. Nothing further occurred. It made Amos uncomfortable, but not to the point that he complained about it. He did not pay much attention to it. It was not until decades later, when the Cantor was fired over similar allegations, that Amos realized that the Cantor's behavior was inappropriate. Although Amos thought that the Cantor was strange, it did not affect his feelings about religion. When he read about Priests committing similar offenses, he realized that every religion has its predators.

Amos knew that Bar Mitzvahs were a major milestone for the Jewish community in Cologne. Unlike many American Bar Mitzvahs, his was celebrated simply. His parents brought crackers, herring, and two bottles of vodka to the Temple for the celebration. The usual crowd of about twenty or thirty congregants was present on a Saturday morning when the ceremony took place. Most of his family was not alive, and the surviving relatives from abroad did not attend. No specific friends attended. It was considered a somber occasion. He kept the tallis for his entire life, the fringed shawl he wore at his Bar Mitzvah, which survived his many moves over the years. Looking back on the occasion as an adult, he was gratified that he had accomplished this rite of passage. It made him proud to be a Jew.

As much as Amos's father wanted Amos to think of himself as a socially conscious German, the fact that he was Jewish could not always be ignored. When Amos was about thirteen or fourteen years old, he had a fight in school with a classmate who called him a "dirty Jew." The boy said those words to Amos in front of their entire school class. The teacher heard the words too, went over to the boy, and hit him in the face. The boy started to cry. Amos was emotionally hurt by this incident. This was among the few times that he had an openly negative experience as a Jew. By the end of the year, the boy was expelled from school. Amos felt that the event played a major role in the boy's expulsion. The other children never mentioned the incident. It was as if it never happened.

On another occasion, around the same time, one of the gym teachers hit Amos because he was angry with him. Amos could not remember if the teacher was angry because Amos was not running fast enough, or if he said something that the teacher did not like, or both. Amos went home and told his parents what had happened. At that point in Amos's life, Amos's father felt emboldened to go to the school. The next day, his father confronted the gym teacher at the school in front of Amos. His father was quite angry and told the teacher that he could never do this again to his son. After that, the teacher was more careful with Amos. The teacher was known to have been a Nazi. Somebody in the community had recognized him from when he was a Nazi, there were photographs of him as a Nazi, and he had admitted that he was. The confrontation between Amos's father and the teacher was restorative for both his father and for Amos.

Several years later, that same teacher became the President of the German Track and Field Association and the Vice-President of the National Olympic Committee. He became famous, and there is a Wikipedia page about him. Ironically, the Wikipedia page does not mention that he was a Nazi. Amos was pleased that despite the fact that his father was afraid of German authority figures, he was able to try to protect him, and to take on a parental role, on that occasion. Amos recalled that when he was a young child, his father had forgotten him at a store, and only realized that Amos was not with him when he arrived home and his wife asked where Amos was. Amos was unharmed, but it was one of many examples when Freddie was unable to provide care and protection. That is why this event with the teacher took on particular importance for Amos.

When Amos was fourteen or fifteen years of age, the head of the school called Amos into his office shortly before the middle of the school year. By way of history, the head of the school had also been a Nazi. Amos saw photographs of him in his SS uniform in a book which Amos's father had found. Amos learned, also, that when the head of school was a teacher during the Nazi era, he made the students go outside, stand in line, and practice the Heil Hitler greeting. When Amos went to his office, he told Amos that he heard that he was failing several classes, and that if he failed two of the major classes, he would not be able to continue in the next school year. He told Amos that he was the first Jew in gymnasium after World War II to make it as far as he had. He told Amos that he was smart and he did not understand why he would fail so many classes. He asked Amos if he needed any help, and told him that he did not want him to fail, that he wanted him to graduate on time, and that Amos should get himself together so that he would not fail.

At that time Amos did not think of himself as having the discipline to do well academically. He did not think of himself as a good German or a good student. He did not think that it was important to finish school. For the rest of his gymnasium years, he was a mediocre student in terms of his grades. However, that meeting with the head of the school woke him up, to an extent. He was determined not to fail. Amos respected authority and the head of school's position in the hierarchy. He was frightened that he might not be able to finish at the school. Some part of him did want to succeed, and more than anything, he wanted to leave Germany. In order to leave Germany, he realized that he would have to be successful one way or another.

Other events shaped Amos's worldview. When he was sixteen years of age, he went to New York for a visit. He learned that New York was a good place to be for Jews. He stayed with the aunt who had sent him the Davy Crockett hat years before, whom he called Aunt Lina. She was a cousin of his paternal grandfather, and one of the few relatives Amos's father remembered. Amos's father had visited her in 1959. Freddie spent three months in New York at that time to see if he could emigrate and then bring the family with him. He determined then that he could not, and Amos was not certain why he made that decision. When Amos visited Aunt Lina, she was married but had no children. She lived on Eastern Parkway in Brooklyn, and went into black neighborhoods and sold underpants and socks. She barely spoke any English. While Amos lived with her, she gave him a culture shock. She took him to a show at Radio City Music Hall. Before the show, they were selling popcorn. She asked if he wanted some and bought it for him. The moment he put it in his mouth he almost spit it out. The popcorn in Germany was made with sugar, and the popcorn at Radio City Music Hall was made with salt. While a minor incident, it made him realize how different expectations can be in diverse cultures, with food and everything else.

While in New York, Amos also stayed for a few days with his father's best friend from concentration camp. He lived on Seventh Avenue in Greenwich Village above a store called the Pleasure Chest, which sold sex toys and other sexual objects. He was a homosexual, although Amos did not know it before he stayed with him. He had a bunk bed, and Amos slept on top. He took Amos around New York City. They went to high priced restaurants, one of which had elephant meat on the menu which Amos tried. They went to several clubs. At one of the clubs, Amos saw Bob Dylan performing. It was at that moment that Amos determined that he definitely wanted to return to New York permanently, as he idolized Bob Dylan, a successful Jewish songwriter, performer and author. Amos noticed that his father's friend had postcards in his kitchen of young boys in different stages of undress, which Amos found strange. He gave Amos a watch, and later sent him a two year subscription for Playboy magazine which Amos received when he went back to Germany. When he died in 1979, Amos was living in New York City permanently. Amos went to the funeral, and observed several young men crying. They told Amos that his father's friend had helped them overcome their drug addictions and paid for them to go to college. Years later, when Amos asked his mother why she and his father let him stay with a gay man who was "into" young boys when Amos was sixteen years old, she replied that she wanted him to "get his own experiences." They did not view him as a danger to Amos. They always felt that Amos could take care of himself and make his own decisions. While this gave Amos strength, sometimes it made him feel alone.

During that same trip to New York, Amos visited his father's old friend from Israel, and who originally lived in Cologne, Germany. He had moved to Connecticut to a farm.

Amos became friendly with his daughters, which also made him want to live in New York. They all visited Yale University together. They bought him a sweatshirt with the lettering of Yale University on it. He told them that one day he would work at Yale University, and they all laughed. When he became a Professor at another Ivy League school, some forty years later, he had realized a long ago dream. Amos always believed in himself, even if others found his dreams laughable, or he thought they did.

While Amos was visiting the farm in Connecticut, their ewe was pregnant. Amos had the opportunity to observe the delivery of the sheep, which took place over many hours. He was fascinated by the miracle of it. Later on in life, when he became a doctor, he had an interest in becoming involved in the birth process and in delivering babies, originating, in part, out of his experience on the farm. While on the farm, they showed him, also, how they grew corn. He went into the cornfield. They told him to quickly pick some ears so that they could cook them. He tasted the corn and did not like it because the corn in Germany was thick, yellow and very firm, and the American corn was not. He later learned that the corn he had picked from the fields in Germany was for animal feed, hence the difference. There were many more class differences Amos had to make sense of over time.

These visits took place in the late 1960's. It was a tumultuous time with the Vietnam war raging, which was on everyone's mind. There was political awakening both in the United States and abroad. When Amos returned to Germany, people were becoming involved in protests there regarding various issues, and there was the start of violent protests. When Amos was about sixteen or seventeen, the first violent one he could recall occurred in Cologne. It was against the local Cologne tram authority which had increased prices for students. The protestors derailed the trams and destroyed windows. The police came on horseback and the protesters threw bags of metal ball bearings on the streets so that the horses would slip on them and fall.

The protesters, who were high school students, also protested against new high rise office buildings which were being built in the middle of Cologne. Amos was one of the participants. There was a new IBM building in Cologne. The protestors destroyed all the windows as far up as they could throw. Some of them had slingshots, which reached up to the windows on the ninth floor of the building. These were the type of windows that you could not look through. Amos did not know if anyone had been arrested. Amos's parents knew about these activities, which Amos sometimes participated in, but they did not criticize him. They mostly let him be. His father had a long history of being rebellious as the black sheep of the family. That type of activity was completely normal for his father. These protests went on for about a year. Eventually, university students became involved in the protests in Cologne as well.

During his late teen years, Amos skirted other types of dangers. When Amos was eighteen, he befriended an older Moroccan man who was in his twenties. He claimed to be Jewish, and as it turns out, was clearly involved in the underworld. Amos had just obtained his first car, and he took several trips to Amsterdam with the man in it. They slept in communal areas on ships that had mattresses. The man apparently bought large amounts of hashish. Amos thought that all of this was adventurous, not realizing at the time how his life could have changed in an instant if he had been arrested.

If they say that a cat has nine lives, Amos must have had at least that as there were so many situations when he could have gone down a path which could have taken him to a very different place than the top of his medical profession. And it was not always that he did not take the path, but that the path did not have permanent consequences for him. Perhaps the biblical quote, "where God guides, he provides" (Isaiah 58:11) has some relevance. Amos and his parents, however, would have argued with the applicability of that quote, particularly in light of the extermination of most of his family members in the Holocaust.

# Chapter Five:
# Amos's Pre-Medical Year
# and Medical School Years

*"A half truth is a whole lie"*
—Jewish Proverb

*"Knowledge is the best merchandise"*
—Jewish Proverb

Luckily for Amos, his intellectual curiosity, hard work, and survival instincts were stronger than his desire to have risky, adventurous experiences involving rebellion, protests or drugs. Perhaps what was even more crucial is that blind luck was with him throughout his life as he managed to dodge possible "bullets."

Amos graduated gymnasium in 1968, at age eighteen, and at that point decided to become a doctor. His father would have preferred that he become a lawyer, but that was not Amos's inclination although he would have made an excellent lawyer. He had a sense of justice, charisma, verbal and written skills, assertiveness, persistence, and an entrepreneurial bent, all of which would have made him successful if he had chosen that route. Amos recognized that studying medicine would be intellectually challenging and would enable him to travel to wherever his skills were needed, whereas law would have been more confining, especially in Germany as a Jew. He was interested in food and cooking as well, but he did not believe that he could make the kind of living he wanted to with that career course at that time.

Medical school in Germany was free. Amos would have been unable to attend otherwise, and the trajectory of his life would have been completely different. He was not accepted into the medical school in Cologne right away. For one year, he enrolled in natural sciences courses at the University of Bonn, the birthplace of Beethoven, and at that time the capital of Germany, approximately twenty minutes South of Cologne. Amos was permitted to take the same classes as the medical students took during their first year. They were similar to pre-med classes in the United States.

Amos left his parent's home in the suburbs permanently, and squatted with other people in unoccupied buildings, so that he could live closer to the University. When Amos was nineteen years old and his sister was fourteen years old, she left their parent's home to live in a commune for about a year. His parents never discussed with Amos how they felt about his sister leaving at such a young age. Amos said his entire immediate family lived in a "white-washed world of denial." His parents accepted what his sister did. Amos never discussed it with his sister, or he does not remember it. After the commune, Amos's sister moved into an apartment for a few months with Amos, which he had rented in Cologne. That arrangement did not work out, as the layout of the apartment was such that they had to walk through one bedroom to get to the other, and, thus, there was no privacy. Amos left that apartment and moved into an apartment in Cologne of his father's brother, who had died. It was a tiny, studio apartment. He lived there until he left Germany at the age of twenty seven. His sister never returned home, and did not live with him again. (She ended up attending art school, and later wrote books, worked on Amos's website, organized medical conferences, managed and owned real estate, ran a farm, and became a mother and grandmother. She remained independent, difficult, and rebellious, and had achievements in her own right).

Amos made another attempt to get accepted into medical school after he completed his natural sciences classes. The University of Cologne mistakenly sent out three times the amount of letters of acceptance to students as it could accommodate. Instead of sending acceptances to one hundred fifty students, they sent out letters to about five hundred. Amos was one of the accepted students. The University of Cologne was sued by several of the students for this. Eventually, as part of the resolution of the lawsuit, the University had to accept all five hundred students.

Amos, however, did not want to wait for the resolution of the lawsuit. This is another instance where Amos's father was able to successfully advocate for him. This time, it was his greatest performance. Freddie went by himself to meet with the Dean of the medical school to urge him to take Amos into the medical school immediately. After the meeting, Freddie told Amos that the Dean said that Amos should go to the office of the University the next day. He was to tell them that the Dean sent Amos to be accepted into the medical school.

When Amos later asked his father what he told the Dean, Freddie replied that he told the Dean several things. Before

Freddie went to speak with the Dean, Freddie researched and found out that the Dean had been a Nazi. He discovered that the Dean had obtained his jobs and advanced in his career because the two people who were ahead of him were fired under the Hitler regime because they were Jewish. Freddie threatened to expose the Dean as not everyone knew he was a Nazi. The second thing he told the Dean is that he was born and raised in Cologne, and that he had to leave Cologne before he went to university. He told the Dean that he had always wanted to be a doctor, but could not be one because the Nazis had taken over. He said that after Amos was born in Israel, he returned to Cologne so that his son could fulfill his dream of being a doctor. He told the Dean that this was not about giving Amos the right to be a doctor, but, at the very least, it would give him the opportunity to prove himself. Some of this story was embellished as Freddie never wanted to be a doctor. In any event, he achieved his goal.

The next day, Amos arrived early in the morning at the University, and was greeted by a man behind a desk. He asked Amos to show him his study book. Every student had a study book for each semester which stated what school the student was in, and which classes the student took. Amos had taken natural sciences classes because he wanted to study medicine. Amos gave the man the study book. The man turned around to a wall behind him, and looked up at the wall which contained many neat rows with dozens of round seal stamps. He found a round seal stamp, he took the study book, he crossed out the natural sciences seal with a pen, and put a new seal stamp next to it. When Amos looked at the study book, he saw that it was a medical school seal stamp. Amos always thought that it was bizarre to see the ease by which your life could change with a different seal. He stated that this was typical for Germany with its emphasis on bureaucracy, meaning inflexible rules, regulations, and procedures to keep order. He noted, ironically, that this reminded him of how different stars or tattoos assigned Jews to different fates in concentration camp. Many of Amos's analyses of situations harkened back to the Holocaust experiences of the Jews. His mind automatically went there.

After Amos was accepted into medical school, and had started his classes, he realized that his challenges were just beginning because the school had to accept all five hundred students in a class that only accommodated one hundred fifty people. Hundreds of students had to stand each day in order to attend the class. Amos, who was always industrious, arrived at 6:00 a.m. for an 8:00 a.m. class in order to obtain seats for himself and his friends. He looked at the situation with the eyes of an entrepreneur, and realized that something was missing that he could take advantage of. Many students could not attend because of the overflow. Amos took written notes of every class and always sat in the first row. Because he made himself highly visible, the professors had the opportunity to know him well, which helped. He diligently mimeographed his notes, put them in booklets, and sold them to the students. He learned more that way because he had to type the notes correctly, and he had to do a little research before he completed his notes. The professors and students knew Amos performed this service. Amos continued to stand out in the crowd, this time not only because he was a Jew, but for providing a useful service that many could benefit from and for his industriousness.

At the end of the first year, and the following year, the medical students were required to take exams, which they called "weed out" exams. The medical schools could not accommodate all students during the clinical years after five semesters. After one year, a lot of students were eliminated. The next three semesters were arduous because he commenced difficult courses in anatomy, physiology and pharmacology. He also had to take a chemistry lab for the first time. The German Professor for the chemistry lab had just returned from the United States, he had missed getting a Nobel Prize, although he was close to getting it, and he was a frustrated researcher. He decided to give the students an entrance examination into the chemistry lab. The students told him that this new requirement was ridiculous because they wanted to be taught something before they were tested. He told the students he could not care less what they thought.

The medical students staged a strike. Their demand was that they had to be accepted into the lab first, and then after being taught, they could be tested. Amos was one of the leaders, and the Professor knew it. The medical students won. They were all accepted into the chemistry lab. However, the Professor did not forget Amos's role in it, and specifically selected Amos for criticism. Whenever the Professor taught the class, he asked Amos the most difficult questions to see if he could answer them. Amos, who welcomed challenges, decided to become a good student at that point. He determined that when someone is out to get you, you have to be better than everyone else. He passed the final examination with flying colors and a top grade. The gymnasium years of mediocre grades, a lack of focus and direction, and little effort, were over.

The years of protests, including breaking windows in buildings, were over too, but Amos became politically involved in a different way in medical school. Amos was not a member of any political student group. He leaned toward a left-wing Communist student group, which mirrored the politics of his parents, particularly that of his father. In 1969, Amos started running in elections to become a member of the school parliament. However, Groucho Marx was Amos's true hero, not Karl Marx. Each of the faculties had a certain number of student representatives. Amos ran on the platform that he would get a Coca-Cola soda machine in the student lounge in the Anatomic Institute. He received enough votes and won. He remained in the student parliament for the remainder of medical school. At one point he became the vice president of the student parliament, continuing the fight to protect students' rights.

Early in his medical school years, in 1970, Amos again skirted danger. At that time, Amos had a girlfriend who had moved to Berlin. Amos visited her there. She had become involved with the left wing movement, which Amos was also a part of in Cologne. Her father was a director of a major pharmaceutical company in Leverkusen, Germany where Amos had visited her several times. Previously, she had lived with her family in what Amos considered to be a castle. When Amos went out with her in Cologne, before she moved to Berlin, her father tried to convince her not to spend time with Amos. Her father felt that Amos was too left wing, and, as if that were not bad enough, was a Jew. Amos learned that her father had been a high ranking Nazi in World War II. In December of 1970, Amos made plans to go for a ski vacation with her in the Alps. They had plans to meet in Cologne. About a week before, when Amos telephoned her at the commune where she lived, he was unable to reach her. She did not respond to his calls. The people who picked up the telephone did not know where she went. Amos was quite disturbed.

In mid-January, Amos finally heard from his girlfriend. She called and simply told Amos that she had to disappear. She asked Amos if she could borrow his car. Amos was always very generous, and even if people did not treat him well, he continued to give them what they asked for. When he said yes to her request, she said that she would send someone over, and that he should park the car in a certain spot in Cologne and leave the keys. The car was picked up. Amos did not know by whom. Several weeks later, there was a bombing at a United States barracks in southern Germany which was attributed to terrorist activities. Shortly afterwards, she called Amos and told him where he could find his car, and that he could pick it up. She told him that he was fortunate because "they did not use his car." Amos said that he did not know what she meant by that statement, and, as was characteristic for him, he did not ask many questions, although he must have had his suspicions. Shortly afterwards she was arrested. Amos learned from the police, who questioned him one time, that she had joined the Baader-Meinhof Group, a West German far-left militant organization, that she had gone underground, and that she was underground when she asked him to use his car. Her father hired one of the top lawyers. She stayed out of prison because of her father's connections, and because she testified against the Baader-Meinhof Group. Amos saw her several times afterwards both in Germany and in New York.

Amos was attracted to wealthy people with leftist views, the best of all worlds for him at the time. Such people had the political views of Amos's family, but a lifestyle which allowed for much more comfort. Amos had been trained by his father to live on the edge, to not judge people, and to consort with people who had questionable ethics. Amos repeated this mistake many times in his life. Although he felt it made his life interesting, it was blind luck which prevented him from suffering some of the consequences of those questionable alliances.

There was another time when Amos barely avoided danger while he was in medical school. In Germany, even medical students had three months vacation in the summer, and according to Amos, Germans took their vacations seriously. In the Summer of 1972, Amos went for a three month trip with his two best friends in a small Volkswagen car. They drove first to what was then Yugoslavia, and slept in barns. One night the Yugoslavian police arrested them at a barn and brought them to a police station because they had not registered their stay overnight, which was required. They were released only after they gave the police a bribe of the equivalent of one hundred Deutsche Marks.

They continued on to Turkey by crossing the mountains between Yugoslavia and Greece. They lost their way on unpaved roads, and after approximately six hours of driving, they were stopped by soldiers. The soldiers drew their guns, and searched their Volkswagen car. It turns out that Amos and his friends had mistakenly driven into Albania, which at that time was a closed communist country with no tourism. People could not enter or leave that country except once or twice per year for soccer games. The Albanian soldiers could speak only in the Albanian language. After spending a night in detention, the Albanian soldiers released them. Amos believes that the soldiers did so because the soldiers realized they they did not have bad intentions.

Amos and his friends drove to Istanbul, Turkey next where they met other friends from medical school. They decided to travel all together. They had been staying in a hostel with bunk beds. Amos and his two friends left for another Turkish city where they were supposed to meet those other friends. One friend never arrived. When Amos returned to Germany at the end of the Summer, he learned that the friend had been arrested by Turkish Police at the hostel. The police found hashish in the friend's possession. A German girl had dropped the hashish into his bag during the raid. Nonetheless, Amos's friend spent two years in a Turkish prison under horrific conditions. The friend returned to Germany after that and finished medical school. Amos realized that he could have easily been the one that ended up in prison.

While in Turkey, Amos and his friends became aware that something had happened at the Munich Olympic Games but they could not find out details easily because all of the newspapers were in Turkish. Eventually, after many days, they were able to access a newspaper in English. They learned that eleven Israeli Olympic team athletes had been kidnapped and slaughtered during the episode, along with a German police officer, by a Palestinian terrorist group. Amos said that if he had been in Germany and had experienced all of those days of pain during that crisis, the Munich massacre, he would have felt even more traumatized by the event. By being in Turkey and away from the news, he was insulated from some of the pain. It was on that occasion that he realized that having access to the news at all times may not always be positive.

His years in medical school reflected the times in simpler ways as well. The biggest event occurred on Wednesday afternoons when the university students did not have classes. Thousands of students congregated in the largest meeting room of the University. They watched movies, including "spaghetti Westerns." For Amos, this was an introduction to American culture. Some students smoked hashish, while others "made out."

In 1970, Amos did an anatomy rotation for a semester, which sparked his curiosity. While on vacation, Amos volunteered to work in the Anatomic Institute in Cologne. Amos worked with a Professor of Anatomy who, before the war, had travelled to the rainforests of Indonesia. He brought back newly discovered species, including slices of large worms. It was Amos's job each day to take a slice of the worm, to project the shadow of the slice on photography paper, to take the imprint of the slice, to put thin wax over it, to cut out the outline of that slice of worm, and then, eventually, to put all of the slices together to recreate the worm. Amos thought these tasks were entertaining. He valued that he had to be meticulous. He was thrilled by the fact that he was the first one to see worms that nobody had described in the past.

While he performed the work, he had to go to the basement of the Institute where the slices were stored. Amos discovered an area with skulls which had labels such as Gypsy, Eastern European Jew, Jewish Midget, and Black. Clearly these were left over from the Nazi era. Amos was too frightened to ask what they were used for as he went into the area where they were housed without permission to be there. Decades later, Amos read in a German newspaper about a scandal involving racially labelled skulls, one of which was that of a Polish worker, and that experiments were conducted on those people. The skulls Amos observed were probably of individuals who had been executed during World War II. To this day, Amos cannot read about experiments on humans which were conducted during that period as it is too painful for him.

Amos had a close Jewish friend who was several years ahead of him in medical school. By the time Amos was in his last years in medical school, his friend had already finished his radiology residency and was a physician in radiology at a large radiological institute in Cologne. The Chief of that institute had significant Nazi ties in the past. During Amos's last years in medical school, he commenced working on his doctoral thesis with that Jewish friend at that radiological institute. Amos developed his scientific interests at that time, as he spent several years in the basement of that institute examining thousands of patient's charts and collecting data on two different kinds of radiation treatment for breast cancer. Eventually, Amos finished his thesis on radiation therapy for breast cancer after he completed medical school. He defended the thesis, and became a doctor of medicine. At that time, in radiology, all of the pictures had to be hand developed, whereas today most of it is done electronically. Amos's friend wanted him to specialize in radiology, and although Amos seriously considered it during his rotating internship, he finally decided to be involved in a more clinical specialty where he was able to have patient contact.

Medical school should have been completed in six years, which for Amos would have been from 1968 through 1974. Amos accelerated his studies, and finished in five and a half years. This was unheard of. He had finished all of his required courses after ten semesters. When he applied to take his final examinations, they rejected him, because they said it had to take a minimum of eleven semesters. Amos then took a semester off to travel. He went to Paris, moved in with a girlfriend for a few months, and attended classes in Paris at a medical school. Even during Amos's time off, he wanted to learn as much as he could. After that semester, he took his final examinations, passed them, and was on his way.

# Chapter Six:
# Amos's Medical Internships and Residencies in Germany

*"Learn from yesterday, live for today, hope for tomorrow. The important thing is not to stop questioning"*
—Albert Einstein

*"There is divine beauty in learning . . . To learn means to accept the postulate that life did not begin at my birth. Others have been here before me, and I walk in their footsteps"*
—Albert Einstein

When Amos finished medical school, he had to go for interviews for several rotating internships that lasted four to six months. Among the first of the interviews was by the Chief of Surgery at a large institution. Amos sat down with him, he looked over Amos's curriculum vitae, and then proceeded to ask him several questions. He asked him where he went to school, and Amos told him in Cologne. He asked him where his father was from, and Amos told him Cologne. He asked him where he went to first grade, and Amos answered in Cologne. Then he finally asked him where he was born, and Amos answered Haifa, Israel. That information was on the curriculum vitae.

The Chief of Surgery then said to Amos, "so you are a Jew." Amos said "yes." He then said that Amos would be the first Jew to work at that hospital after World War II, and that there had been many Jewish doctors there before the war. He told Amos that "we have nothing against Jews." That single sentence, at the end of a long interview, was imprinted in Amos's brain. Amos clearly knew that people in Germany were against the Jews and had killed them en masse. Amos found it inconceivable that all of a sudden, after World War II, nobody had anything against the Jews, when, in fact, they probably did. That occasion was among the first times that Amos made the conscious decision to "show the Germans what Jews could do," and to leave Germany and move to a place where being Jewish was not different from being anyone else. From the time Amos was sixteen years old, he began to think about leaving Germany to be part of a more all-encompassing society, where people were not considered to be different because of their religion. After that interview, Amos felt that yearning even more acutely.

There was another time during his internship years when Amos became convinced that he would have to leave Germany. There was a newspaper article Amos read about a house painter who was employed by a Catholic hospital. The house painter had been fired from his job. He challenged the termination of his employment in court. The hospital found out that the house painter had been divorced and fired him because they believed that people who were divorced were against Catholic values and could not work in a Catholic hospital. The majority of the hospitals in and around Cologne were either Catholic or Protestant. The chiefs of the individual medical services were chosen, partially, because they had the same religion, and they could not be divorced. Amos felt that such views were unacceptable. He recognized, also, that since he was Jewish and there was no Jewish hospital in Germany, he would never be able to "move up the chain" because of his religion. In fact, many of the physicians who had the position of Oberarzt were physicians from Muslim countries such as Iran, Turkey, Syria and Lebanon. They knew they would never be able to move up to a chief position because of their religion, and Amos knew that such discrimination also applied to himself.

In Amos's first internship rotation, he rotated through a small village hospital in Bedburg, Germany, which was about forty five minutes west of Cologne. At one point Amos's father told him that his great grandparents used to live and work in that village as horse traders. When Amos asked his father where the great grandparents were buried, he told him that they must be at the Jewish cemetery there. Amos began to inquire as to where the Jewish cemetery was located. An older man told Amos that he remembered where it was. He took Amos about a mile from the hospital. They arrived at a mile-wide, deep coal pit. The man pointed to the middle of the coal pit and said that the cemetery was there. Amos felt destroyed by that information. He thought, "this is not a place for me to be."

The disrespect Amos felt took place at the hospital as well. The hospital was run by nuns in nun's garb. They were extremely tough, and they treated Amos dismissively. He felt that they did not take him seriously. At one point the nun superior called Amos to her office to complain that he had prescribed birth control pills for some of the Filipino nurses who had been working there. She told Amos that birth control was against the Catholic Church beliefs and he should stop doing that. She then pointed to the wall where there was a one foot large cross with Jesus on it. That kind of cross was located throughout the hospital in each room and in the hallways. She told him that the Lord Jesus is against birth control. Amos, without skipping a beat, and without regard to consequences, told her that he knew about Jesus because he was a Jew, also, and that he was not certain Jesus would be against birth control. The nun became highly upset, and shortly thereafter, Amos was asked to leave the hospital. They told him that he did not follow the Catholic philosophy. Amos was not unhappy about leaving.

Soon thereafter, Amos started a rotating internship in anatomic pathology. It involved performing many autopsies and looking at pathologic slides at the City Hospital in Leverkusen, Germany. After Amos completed his four month internship, he decided to stay for another year in a residency in pathology, from 1975 through 1976, even though he knew that he did not want to remain in the field of pathology forever. The reason for his decision was that many major university hospitals required that a doctor spend several years in what they considered basic rotations, such as pathology or anatomy, before being accepted into a better residency program.

In 1976, after his pathology residency, but before his anesthesia residency, Amos travelled to the United States. That trip coincided with celebrations of the 200th anniversary of the existence of the United States. Amos had a girlfriend in Connecticut whom he stayed with. He decided that he would move to the United States the following year.

From 1976 to 1977, Amos did a residency in anesthesia at the Weyertal Hospital in Cologne. One day, during that residency, a red-headed pregnant woman came into the hospital.

She was the sister of Amos's best friend in gymnasium, and they had recognized one another when she was admitted to the hospital. She was bleeding extensively, and was extremely ill. Amos delivered the baby. The mother died quickly after the baby was born. It turned out that she had an acute fatty liver, a rare but often lethal condition in pregnancy. That single event made Amos want to go into the field of obstetrics and gynecology. Amos realized that despite pregnancy being a joyful event for a majority of women, it could also be lethal, and that doctors could make a difference in saving lives.

During that year, Amos suffered from another traumatic incident when he was "on call" as a first year anesthesia resident. One evening, Amos was called to access the condition of a Turkish woman who had undergone a thyroid operation earlier that day. She had difficulty breathing, with a stridor, which is an abnormal, high-pitched sound caused by a blockage in the throat or voice box. Amos called the Oberarzt, an experienced Doctor who specialized in anesthesia, who was at home and on call. Amos explained the situation, and the Doctor told him not to worry, and that her symptoms were normal after thyroid surgery. Later that evening, the woman had a cardiac arrest. Amos tried to intubate her, but he could not because her windpipe had become completely swollen. She died. The incident made Amos realize how crucial the quality of care is. He stated that they should have intubated the women earlier that evening, and that they should have realized that she was on her way to not being able to breathe. Amos felt that they were responsible for her death, and it weighed on him. Throughout his career, especially in his supervisory roles, that event went through his mind continuously when he analyzed adverse outcomes in cases. He always looked at all of the angles to see how to improve future care.

During that year, Amos befriended the second in command of Obstetrics. However, the Chief of Obstetrics, at that time, was an older Professor who had Nazi ties in the past. Amos believed that despite his interest in that field, that fact was another reason for him to move to the United States. Although Amos was accepted into the ob/gyn residency at the hospital in Germany, he did not accept it. Amos applied to several hospitals in the United States, and he was invited for interviews. One hospital was in Newark, New Jersey. When Amos disembarked from the train in Newark, he had to walk through poor, slum neighborhoods, which had been virtually destroyed years earlier from the riots, and never restored, in order to get to the interview. That was something that he had never seen before, not even in post-war Cologne. He decided not to work at that hospital because it was too "foreign" for him. He also went for an interview for an anesthesia residency at a hospital in Brooklyn, and was accepted. He did that residency for one year. The ob/gyn residencies were too competitive to apply for in the United States at that time, so he bided his time.

It took Amos some time to decide to forgo the opportunity in Germany, especially since he had decided that he wanted to become an ob/gyn. Amos's mother seemed to be happy that he wanted to leave Germany. She was quietly supportive of the decision. Amos's father was also supportive of the idea. Not all of Amos's friends understood why he wanted to leave Germany. Some of his friends moved to Israel, but everyone else stayed in Germany. Amos did not feel guilty at all about leaving his family or about leaving Germany. He wanted to move forward in his life and to advance in his career. He wanted to develop skills which were scientifically advanced, to be involved in research, and to deliver as many babies as he could. He also wanted mentors whom he could admire. He did not believe that he could achieve any of those goals in Germany as the professors in Germany, in his view, were third tier. The first two tiers, he explained, had been killed off or left Germany.

# Chapter Seven:
# Amos's Medical Residencies
# in New York

*"When a stranger sojourns with you in your land, you shall not do him wrong. You shall treat the stranger who sojourns with you as the native among you, and you shall love him as yourself, for you were strangers in the land of Egypt. I am the Lord your God"*

—Leviticus 19:33-34

Amos arrived in the United States in June of 1977. He moved in with his cousin Murray, who lived in Canarsie, Brooklyn. Murray's father was Amos's father's second cousin. He had survived the war in Israel and emigrated to the United States with Murray in the mid 1950's. For the first three and a half years of Amos's life, when he lived in Israel, he spent time with Murray, but did not really remember him.

Cousin Murray was a teacher by profession. He owned the building in which they lived. Amos rented the basement apartment, and Murray lived one floor above. Murray was a kind man, but he held political views which were the opposite of Amos's. Murray believed in right wing and conservative politics, he supported the United States' involvement in the Vietnam War, and he was a racist. Murray was not interested in the arts and high culture. Amos remembers going with him to the Star Wars movie in one of the biggest movie theatres in Brooklyn. Because of their differences, there was a limit to how close they could become, but it was a comfort to Amos to live near a relative, especially when he first arrived in New York.

On the floor above where Murray lived, there was a renter. He was a Jewish man from Poland in his fifties who had survived the Holocaust. He reminded Amos of a butcher. He had rough facial features, he was burly, and he performed some kind of manual job. He often sat outside on the stoop of the building. One evening he told Amos a story, which he said he had never told anybody before. The story made a strong impression upon Amos. He said that he was a teenager when he was rescued from Auschwitz concentration camp. After he recovered from his illnesses, and moved back to Poland, he banded together with other teenagers in Poland. They identified SS guards who had worked in the concentration camps. They found out where they lived. They went out at night, massacred them and their families, robbed their houses, and then burned their houses down. This took place for about six to twelve months, shortly before he emigrated to the United States. He moved to the United States to get away from Poland. The man expressed to Amos that he never felt guilty about what he and the others did, and he had no regrets whatsoever. He said that they received what they deserved and that their families participated in the evil of Auschwitz. After Auschwitz, he explained, he and the other survivors were all severely damaged and their ethical compasses were non-existent. When he arrived in the United States, he felt that it was a different time in his life and he was able to begin life anew.

Amos understood him and what had happened to him. When Amos was growing up in Germany, there were several trials against SS men in Cologne and in Dusseldorf, another German city. Amos's father was obsessed with attending the trials. Freddie told Amos, later, that he had carried a knife with him on several occasions, and was planning to attack and to kill the defendants. Amos had sympathy for those feelings and could understand why tormentees wanted to attack their tormentors. There was nothing unusual for Amos about that expression of emotion.

Once Amos started his residency at a hospital in Brooklyn, there were numerous culture shocks. When Amos received his first paycheck, he had no idea what to do with it. Cousin Murray told him to deposit it in a bank. When Amos went to the bank, they told him that in order to open an account, he had to have a social security number, which he did not have. It took Amos some time to obtain that number. In the meantime, Cousin Murray deposited Amos's money in his own bank account.

Food was always very important to Amos, as an interest and as a source of comfort. Initially, because he was so used to German food, he could not adapt to American food. He missed his own cuisine. Amos used some of his cash, and bought a car to drive to work at the hospital. When he drove through different neighborhoods to get there, he observed many areas in complete disrepair, which was the ultimate culture shock. There was a larger divide economically between the rich and poor in the United States than in Germany.

As far as culture shocks he experienced during his work at the hospital, Amos recalled that an anesthesia attending physician re-used disposable syringes on different patients in order to save money. The attending explained to Amos that he was only injecting medications so that he was not affecting patients. Amos knew that this was clearly not true, and was something which did not happen in Germany.

Another culture shock for Amos was the sport of baseball. In October of 1977, the staff at the hospital was watching the World Series. That sport was completely new to Amos. He observed that the players looked unfit, overweight, and that all they did was swing a wooden stick. During one of the games, a player hit three home runs in one game. It appeared to be a "big deal" to others, but Amos did not understand why. It turned out that the player was Reggie Jackson, who helped the Yankees to win the World Series in 1977. Amos later learned about all of the rules, statistics and players of American sports, and could intelligently converse with fans about it. He knew that it was important to relate to hospital personnel and patients about sports as it was an important part of American culture. He remained a fan of international soccer, which interest he shared with his father in his youth.

In Amos's personal life during that period, he tried to keep up a relationship with his girlfriend who lived in Connecticut. Her grandparents were Holocaust survivors, and her father was Amos's father's best friend in Israel. Toward the end of the first six months that Amos worked in the hospital in Brooklyn, the relationship fizzled, and then ended, despite their shared family histories.

His work in the hospital took up all of his time and energy. In early 1978, Amos woke up one morning, and there was over two feet of snow outside of the building where he lived. He could not open the screen door. Amos told Murray that he was on call that night. Murray told him to stay home as there was no way he could get to work. There were no cars or people on the street. Amos felt responsible to get to work. He dressed, made his way out of the building, and walked to the subway. He had to take three different subways to get to one of the two hospitals he worked at. It took him four hours to get to work. When he finally arrived, the resident who was on call the night before could not believe that he was able to get there. That resident was not permitted to leave until someone relieved him. He left immediately after Amos arrived. The next morning, no one came to relieve Amos. Nobody came the day after that, or the day after that. On day three, the National Guard came and brought some food to the hospital. In the meantime, Amos and staff had broken into the vending machines to eat. It turned out that Amos spent a total of four days in the hospital until he was relieved.

During the residency, there was always an attending physician with the residents. One day the assigned attending physician did not arrive at work. Everybody started to panic. The attending physician from the night before had to stay at the hospital until another attending arrived. The next day, Amos found out that the attending physician who never arrived had committed suicide. He was a foreign medical graduate from Haiti. Amos felt a special kinship towards other foreign medical graduates. He remembered the Haitian doctor fondly as a nice, responsible person. Amos learned that the Doctor went to a hotel, and started an intravenous fluid drip on himself with drugs that made him sleep and stopped his breathing. The Doctor had failed his board examination for the third time. He was told by the Chief that he had to leave his job. He had a family and two small children. The suicide was traumatizing for everyone. It was not the first time that someone Amos knew had committed suicide. Amos recalled thinking that he was determined not to ever let that happen to him. He vowed to himself that he would work as hard as he could to complete his board examinations on time and get his license.

Shortly thereafter, Amos applied to take the medical licensing examination in Connecticut. He could not take the examination in New York at that point because of the requirement that the applicant had to have completed a minimum of one year of residency before obtaining the New York license. Amos took the examination in Hartford, Connecticut. Amos admitted that there were some questions that he did not understand. He looked over at someone else's test paper whom he did not know. There was no logic to that act because he could not have known if that person knew the answers any better than he did. The proctor caught him and told him not to look over at someone else's paper or he would be disqualified. Amos told the proctor that he would not do that again. Amos was deeply ashamed that he had done this. He explained that his ethics and confidence improved later in his life. This was another time where he was saved from what could have been a catastrophe. He passed the examination and became licensed in the State of Connecticut in 1978. When he finished one year of residency, he applied and became licensed as a physician in New York. It was early in his residency to obtain the license in New York, but he was determined to move on in his career quickly.

During Amos's anesthesia residency in Brooklyn, the Chief of Anesthesia told Amos that he had "wonderful hands" for anesthesia, as Amos was able to perform difficult spinal and epidural anesthesias. He encouraged Amos to become an obstetric anesthesiologist, and offered him the position of Chief of Obstetric Anesthesia. In order to accept the offer, Amos would have had to do a one year internship in obstetrics and gynecology to better understand the specialty. With the help of the Chief, Amos applied for the ob/gyn residency program at a Brooklyn hospital. Amos did not hear back from them. One day, Amos went home after having been "on call." There was a message on his answering machine from a secretary at the Brooklyn hospital where he had applied. The message was that he had been invited for an interview that day, and that he had missed it. Amos did not know why he had never received the message about the interview. He called back, and dressed immediately in his best and only suit, which was green corduroy. He wore a turtleneck sweater instead of a button down shirt. Amos had a bohemian side to him, and, even for an interview, could not bring himself to wear conservative attire. Although Amos had been "on call" the night before, he pushed himself to go to the interview. It was sheer luck that he was home that day to get the message.

Amos was interviewed by a doctor who was about to become the Chief of ob/gyn at the Brooklyn hospital. The doctor was present at the hospital that day specifically to interview applicants. He asked Amos, among other things, how many babies he had delivered. Amos replied that he delivered so many babies it was difficult to count, but probably in the range of forty or fifty. In fact, Amos had not delivered any babies up to that point. The soon-to-be Chief offered Amos the job, which he accepted. Amos was the first resident he hired in his new capacity. The ob/gyn residency commenced in June of 1978.

Ironically, during Amos's first two weekends "on call" at the new job, he delivered approximately forty babies. The hospital where he did his residency was large and mainly served poor people. Amos recalled that it was chaotic and disorganized, and that there was barely any supervision of residents. He recalled that there were many pregnant women who died on a regular basis and that nobody paid much attention to it. That situation, although in many ways not optimal, provided Amos with an opportunity to learn and to get a tremendous amount of experience because of the sheer volume of deliveries he participated in.

At that time, fetal monitoring and ultrasound were not used on a widespread basis. There was no epidural anesthesia available for women in labor. Women labored in the same room, and there were continuous screams from women during the painful portions of their labor. Amos thought that the conditions at the hospital were akin to those in a third world country, and were so different from what had been available in Germany where medical care, in his view, was far superior. Amos continually treated women with advanced medical conditions which could have easily been taken care of if they had been seen by a doctor earlier on in their pregnancies.

The hospital building was unsanitary as well. There were cockroaches in every single room. During one weekend that Amos remained in the hospital, he took transparent adhesive tape and taped every cockroach that ran over a life size mirror. By the end of the weekend, there were hundreds of cockroaches, many of which were still wiggling under the tape. On Monday, when Amos went home, he was called back by the Director of the Service. She told Amos that she was "grossed out" by this. Amos, with his typically direct speech and offbeat sense of humor, told her that she should have been more "grossed out" by the cockroaches that were in the patient's rooms than what he had done to illustrate a point. He told her that he was helping because he was decreasing the cockroach population. A few days later, when Amos looked at the cockroaches under the tapes, he saw that when they died, they delivered babies, so that tiny cockroaches were still wiggling under the tape. He also recalled that during a cesarean section surgery, a cockroach had fallen into the women's open womb, and the surgical team had difficulties finding it. These were the conditions they all worked under.

There were other dangers at that hospital as well. Amos recalled that one time he was delivering the baby of a young African American teenager. Her boyfriend was present in the delivery room. As she was pushing, Amos was about to give her an injection to relieve her pain. Her boyfriend saw Amos with a long needle, and asked him what he was doing. Amos explained that he was giving her an injection. He asked Amos where. Amos pointed and said, "down there, where she had pain, at her perineum near the vagina." The boyfriend pulled a gun, pointed it at Amos, and said, "you ain't putting that needle into her pussy." The entire team left the room, with the delivering mother still on the table, and with her boyfriend pointing the gun at Amos. The baby was close to having to be delivered. As Amos was delivering the baby, alone, the boyfriend had the gun pointed at him the entire time.

Eventually, security at the hospital arrived. They did not have guns. The boyfriend hid his gun behind his back. As security was escorting him out of the room, he yelled at Amos, "I am waiting for you outside. You are a dead man if anything happens to her." This incident occurred shortly after the newly arrived Chief of Trauma Surgery, a Swede, was shot and killed by one of his patients in his office at that hospital. Despite the environment, Amos recalled that he was not afraid. You can never tell with Amos whether his denial runs so deep that he does not feel fear, such that he could not admit it to himself, or if he would never admit to anyone that he felt fear. He used his parents' experiences in concentration camp as a barometer for everything in life, and compared to that, nothing was as serious in his mind.

Some of the dangers at the hospital came from the staff's work ethic. Amos recalled that one time Amos was supervising several women who were in labor, all by himself. He was called to another floor to start an intravenous drip. At hospitals in Germany, the nurses usually started the intravenous drip. When Amos arrived at the floor, there was no intravenous tubing or solution next to the patient. It was 11:00 p.m. When Amos asked the nurse, who was sitting at the desk, to help him to get the solution so that he could quickly start the intravenous, and get back to the women who were in labor on another floor, she responded that she had just painted her fingernails, that they were drying, and that she could not help him until one half hour later. She never got up to help Amos. Amos responded with some curses. The following week, Amos was told by the Chairman of the Department that there was a complaint about him for cursing at a nurse. Amos explained to the Chairman what the nurse had done, or did not do. Amos told him that the nurse was at fault and that she should be reported, not him. Amos was a fighter and believed in justice. The Chairman agreed, but told Amos that he should not lose his temper. Amos always got along well with the hard-working, "salt of the earth," team player types at all levels in the hospital, but he could not tolerate laziness and a bad attitude.

Amos was struck by the reasons some of the patients went to the hospital where he worked. He recalled an occasion when he observed a white man on a stretcher with a bloody drape over his abdomen. His abdomen was open and his bowel was protruding. His stretcher was about to be pushed into the operating room. The police were interrogating him, and Amos heard them asking him if he knew what happened. The man told the police that he was walking on the street, when all of a sudden a helicopter landed next to him and the blades opened his belly. It was clear to everyone that his explanation was not what happened. He was probably cut open with a sharp knife. He looked like someone who was a part of the criminal underworld. Amos thought to himself that he was lucky to be in the United States to experience all of these interesting medical stories. He had just read about a famous pathologist who emigrated to the United States from Israel in the 1950's. When the pathologist was asked why he left Israel, he said that there was only one murder in Israel in the past seven years, and that was not a good basis for his forensic work.

Even though Amos was able to get a prodigious amount of experience at the hospital, and was exposed to many difficult situations which he had to successfully navigate, he was increasingly concerned about the conditions for the doctors, and by extension, for the patients. He became a member of the doctor's union. In 1979, the union organized the first doctor's strike in the United States. The reason for the strike was that the doctors were fighting to be "on call" less frequently for the sake of their patients and their own health.

At that time, the residents had to be "on-call" every other night. It was thirty six hours on, twelve hours off, and another thirty six hours on, etc. The residents were continually exhausted. Amos recalled several resuscitations of patients who were dying. After Amos participated in the resuscitations and was relieved, he fell asleep within ten seconds, in bed, next to the patient who was dying. The strike was successful in that the new rule was that the residents had to be on-call every third night. It was still too much. Years later, because of the Libby Zion case involving a patient who died at a hospital in New York, New York laws were enacted to decrease the workload for residents. Work hour restrictions now govern residency training in all specialties.

Amos's ob/gyn residency was for four years, until 1982. It was his goal to work in an academic center. Amos began to publish papers. During his first year as a resident, he published a paper entitled "One Hundred Years of Tubal Sterilization." At that time, there was no internet, and all of the research had to be done at the University's library with old journals and books. The first doctor who had published about tubal ligation did so one hundred years before Amos did. He chose that topic, in part, because it was the 100th anniversary of that subject matter.

The next paper was a case report which Amos had not originally participated in. It was supposed to be written up by the Chief Resident who left the hospital without writing it. Amos took on the case and published it. This case involved an unusual ectopic pregnancy, which is a pregnancy in which the fetus develops outside of the uterus. Amos published several more papers during his residency, which was more than any other resident during that time period. Because of his willingness to work harder than most people, and his ability to excel doing clinical and academic work, it helped him to get accepted into a maternal-fetal medicine fellowship subsequent to his residency, which provided the basis for his career.

# Chapter Eight:
# Amos's Maternal Fetal Fellowship, Obstetric Group Practice, and Hospital Work: 1982 to 2001

*"All the world is full of suffering. It is also full of overcoming"*
—Helen Keller

*"Adversity has the effect of eliciting talents, which in prosperous circumstances would have lain dormant"*
—Horace

All was not going to be uncomplicated for Amos. A few months after he was accepted into and commenced the maternal-fetal medicine fellowship in the same institution where he did his ob/gyn residency, he was called into the office of an administrator of the hospital. He told Amos that he had to leave because they learned that his residency visa had expired, and that the H-1 visa did not cover his fellowship. Amos had assumed, and was told previously by the hospital, that his visa was sufficient. The Chairman who hired him knew nothing about this. Amos was reassured by the administrator that he had two years to obtain a more permanent visa. Overnight his life was shattered. He could not work without the visa.

Someone in the hospital gave Amos the name of an immigration lawyer. The lawyer told him that the only way to get his job back was to get married. Amos had a girlfriend at the time. She told him that she was not the "marrying kind," but agreed to get married to help him out. They were subsequently married within a week of the firing. Amos was re-hired as soon as he showed the hospital the marriage certificate and application for a green card. Amos and his first wife had a child together, and remained married for seventeen years. They tried to make it work for the sake of their child, but it was not a happy marriage, and it could not survive. They divorced in 2003.

At the end of Amos's residency and the beginning of his fellowship, a new disease called AIDS emerged as a public health threat. The hospital where Amos worked specialized in taking care of HIV/AIDS patients. Two of the doctors with whom Amos worked died from AIDS. One doctor inadvertently stuck herself with a syringe and needle during a resuscitation after she sat on a bed where somebody else had placed a syringe and needle with blood.

When AIDS patients were admitted to the hospital at that time, they were placed into separate rooms. Doctors were only allowed to enter the rooms if they were fully masked and wearing gowns, gloves, and covered shoes. They were required to be fully protected. The first AIDS patient Amos took care of was from Brazil. She had been infected by her husband.

One day, that patient arrived at the hospital and was brought into the operating room. She was about to deliver a breech baby, where the baby's feet were positioned to be delivered first. Amos was called. When he went into the operating room, he realized he was all alone. There was nobody there to help him. All of the staff were afraid of being infected.

Around the same time as that event, and before Amos was dating the woman who later became his first wife, he had a relationship with a nurse/midwife who had just separated from her husband of many years. The husband told her he was gay and could not be with her anymore. Several months into the relationship with Amos, she told him that her husband had been diagnosed with AIDS, and he subsequently died. In those years, nobody understood the dangers of AIDS. Thinking back on that time, Amos felt lucky that he had not contracted AIDS given his work delivering babies of patients with AIDS, and having had an intimate relationship with a woman who had been exposed to AIDS. That is an example of another time he remained unscathed despite the potential danger.

Many times, Amos was exposed to "temptation," but managed to resist it. During Amos's fellowship, one of his fellow residents, who was Haitian, had joined her husband's practice. One day he saw her emerge from a black Mercedes vehicle driven by a black chauffeur, wearing an expensive fur coat. She met Amos on the sidewalk, and said to him, "I am raking in the money and look at you." Amos was wearing dirty scrubs and he had not shaved for several days. She asked him if he wanted to join her practice. She told him he could make more money by doing so. Amos thanked her but declined the invitation as he wanted to remain in academic medicine.

The following year, the woman doctor and her husband were arrested. It turned out that they had opened several abortion mills in Brooklyn and had made millions of dollars. An Assistant District Attorney who was operating under cover went to their practice, told them that she may be pregnant, and asked them to do a pregnancy test. She gave them urine, which was actually urine from her husband. The doctors told her that the test was positive for pregnancy, and that they could do an abortion right away. The Assistant District Attorney had taped the entire interaction. Amos's former colleague and her husband were convicted of fraud. She lost her medical license. It was one of many instances when Amos learned the lesson that "while being unethical could pay a lot of money, it could also get you thrown into prison, or into Hell." Amos determined never to do anything which would interfere with his ethics.

When Amos finished his fellowship in 1984, he joined an obstetric group practice which consisted of the Chairman, two other maternal fetal medicine doctors, and an ob/gyn. The ob/gyn, who was a woman, eventually moved to a Caribbean Island, and some years later, Amos heard that she had committed suicide. Another tragedy involving a person Amos knew well. Amos stayed in the practice for three years.

During that time, he wrote several papers. He worked on the subject that cervical cancer may be associated with HPV, human papillomavirus infection. He spent many months in the electron microscopy laboratory looking at biopsies from cervixes which had abnormal cells. Amos was the first person to find pictures of the HPV virus in the abnormal cervical cells, and he published an article about it. Amos learned decades later that a German professor received a Nobel Prize in medicine for discovering other laboratory techniques about the relationship between HPV infection and cervical cancer. Had Amos persisted with that research, he might have received the prize. Amos mused that life is not necessarily about making a great invention, but about being persistent and continuously exploring the area and expanding upon it. He felt that one of the most important "secrets" of life is that one has to be persistent and continue on a path even when the path does not look promising or you don't realize that you have an important path.

During that time, in 1985, his daughter was born. Amos lived on the Upper West Side of Manhattan, and commuted to Brooklyn each day. After a while, the commute became cumbersome because of his hours. Amos was offered the position of Director of Maternal Fetal Medicine at a community hospital in Manhattan. When Amos told the Chairman at the Brooklyn hospital that he planned to accept that position, the Chairman was disappointed. He told Amos that he was on a path to become a famous professor, and that taking a position at a community hospital would end that progress. Amos did not quite understand what he meant because he thought that becoming a director at a community hospital was something wonderful. It took Amos decades, when he became a full professor at a top medical center in Manhattan, to appreciate what the Chairman meant.

Amos worked at the Manhattan community hospital between 1987 and 2001. During that time, in the late 1980's, the AIDS crisis became prevalent in New York. Amos, as the Director of Maternal Fetal Medicine, met with AIDS activists in Harlem who were protesting against the hospital. They accused the hospital of keeping two different banks of blood, one for black people, and one for white people. They accused the hospital of giving AIDS to Arthur Ashe, the tennis star. AIDS activists staged "die ins" in front of the hospital. They would lie down in the street, and someone would draw chalk around them so that it looked like the entire street was filled with dead people. This mirrored a murder scene when chalk was drawn around a corpse. It was ironic that given his political activities in Germany as a protester, he was now on the other side by virtue of his position in which his goal was to make certain that pregnant women could deliver safely at the hospital. Amos had empathy for the protesters' message, as he understood that racism still existed in the United States. He was the perfect person to try to bring calm to the situation.

Amos faced personal challenges and triumphs during that time period. In 1989, he developed acute appendicitis. He had extensive surgery on his bowels and bladder to repair a perforation of the appendix. That surgery was extremely traumatic for Amos because he realized that he could have died quickly. Nonetheless, he went back to work within two weeks with his wound still open for another four weeks. He then became Interim Chairman of Obstetrics for a few years.

Even though there were painful medical challenges, Amos always made time for some fun. In 1993, Amos received a telephone call in his office during which he was asked to consult on a movie. He was asked to go to the movie set to meet with the director and to review the accuracy of the set. Amos replied, jokingly, that he was a director himself, meaning a medical director, and that they should come to him. He was told that he had to go to the set. Amos was about to hang up the telephone when he asked who the director was, and he was told that it was Ron Howard. Amos was a big fan of the television show Happy Days, so he agreed to go to the movie set. The set was located in one of the most famous buildings on the Upper West Side of Manhattan, the Ansonia, in a large apartment. He met Ron Howard and the female star, Marisa Tomei, who had just won an Oscar award.

Amos was asked to review the script, and he found an error. Marisa Tomei's character was pregnant. She was supposed to be on the telephone, and to then experience bleeding and pain. The script said she had a condition called placenta previa, which is when the placenta attaches to the top of the cervix. Amos knew that placenta previa was associated with painless bleeding, so he changed her condition in the script to abruptio placentae, a detachment of the placenta from the uterus, which is a more dramatic medical event. Her character was supposed to bleed on the chair. Ron Howard asked Amos to place the red coloring on the chair, to indicate where she would have bled.

The next day, the movie shoot was supposed to take place in an old hospital area. Amos was asked to consult there too. During the scene where Marisa Tomei's character was having a caesarean section, Amos observed that the actors did not know how to behave in an operating room. After Amos told Ron Howard, he made Amos do the scene as Marisa Tomei's obstetrician. In the actual movie, Amos scrubbed, and then did a three hundred sixty degree gown dance, which refers to when the doctor comes with his elbows elevated after scrubbing, and the nurse holds the gown for the doctor to slide into with both of his arms. Amos proudly refers to this experience as his short but intense Hollywood career.

There were other traumas for Amos after the good times. In the Fall of 1995, he had to attend a malpractice trial against both him and the hospital in the Bronx. The case involved a woman, who was not Amos's patient, who had her fourth vaginal delivery. There was nothing wrong with the delivery itself. When she went home after the delivery, she claimed that she was unable to walk because her pelvic bone had separated. She accused the hospital, and Amos, as the attending physician, of being responsible for that. It was clearly a nuisance suit. The hospital's investigators had videotaped the woman walking normally on several occasions. When she testified in court, she claimed that she could walk only with a cane and with severe pain. The video showed her shopping, and carrying heavy shopping bags, with no assistance.

The month leading up to the trial and the trial itself were extremely stressful for Amos.

Amos submitted to three days of questioning on the witness stand. Amos's father travelled from Germany to support him, and was present every day at the trial. This was another crucial time when Amos's father was able to sustain and to encourage him, and Amos fully appreciated that. Even though Amos knew that the suit was "bogus," he was not yet a United States citizen, and he felt acutely vulnerable as he recalled what had happened to his parents at the hands of authority figures. The jury decided in Amos's favor. His defense lawyer told him that it was nearly unheard of that a malpractice trial in the Bronx resulted in a defense verdict.

The biggest trial of Amos's life occurred several months later on Martin Luther King's birthday in 1996. He was sitting in the kitchen of his apartment reading a newspaper. He felt tired but did not think much of it as he always worked long hours. He decided to go back to sleep. When he woke up several hours later, he was unable to get out of bed because he could not keep his balance. When he called his then wife, who was with his daughter at her swim meet, he had slurred speech. His wife's cousin picked him up and drove him to the hospital. Amos was diagnosed with a significant thrombotic stroke of the cerebellum at the age of forty-six. Amos spent five days in the intensive care unit and another four days in the hospital. He was taking medication to prevent his blood from clotting. That medication, in and of itself, had the potential for serious side effects. He was unable to go to work for at least six months while he was recovering, and it took him many more years to partially recover. He continued to have slurred speech and poor balance. It took him time to get out of bed in the morning, he could not speak well, he could not give public talks, he could not walk for long distances, and he had to be careful not to fall. He could not take a shower because of his lack of balance. He could not take a bath when he was alone in the apartment. His thoughts during that time were that he was grateful to be alive and to be able to breathe and eat. He took private yoga lessons at home, and had massages, to help him to recover. The doctors were never able to figure out why he had the stroke. He had a blood clot that entered his cerebellum, which is the lower, back part of the brain that manages speech and balance, but nobody knew why that developed.

While he was in the hospital, Amos realized that he might not be able to work as an obstetrician again. When he arrived home from the hospital, he bought himself a computer. At that time, it was highly unusual to own a computer, especially a computer which was attached to the internet. Amos taught himself basic computer language and, shortly thereafter, he started building his own website. He reasoned that if the stroke prevented him from being able to physically perform his job, at the very least, he could share his knowledge with others via the internet. He began to build up pages on his website. In order to make money, he worked with two websites. He answered questions on line, and, at the same time, he took those answers, and expanded upon them on his website.

When he went back to work he could work only part time. He saw ob/gyn patients in his office. The stroke stopped Amos's ascent to become the Chief of the Department of ob/gyn. It prevented him from taking over the job permanently. Amos recalled that he had no choice but to accept his medical condition. It did not make him depressed because he reasoned that he was still alive, and had part of his job.

Amos found that transmitting his medical knowledge through his writings was deeply satisfying. In 1998, he wrote a book with a celebrity about sex in pregnancy. Despite having impaired speech from his stroke, he went to bookstores with the celebrity to speak about the book. His speech was improving, but it was not yet perfect. He later wrote two more books with the celebrity. One was a pregnancy guide for couples, and the other was a book about women's gynecological care at the doctor's office. He also wrote a book with another celebrity about pregnancy and postpartum care. He did not make money from any of these books. It did, however, make him appear more interesting, and showed to his patients and colleagues at the hospital that he had a wide range of interests. Writing the books allowed him to become more versatile on different levels, and he also found that speaking to the general public was satisfying. His writing of the first book shortly after he had the stroke helped him to feel better about himself and allowed his abilities to be expanded to other areas.

That same year, Amos's parents arrived for a visit over the Jewish holidays. Amos learned that his father had a chronic cough for the prior couple of months. He was eighty years old at the time. At Amos's urging, his father had a cat scan upon his return to Germany, and was diagnosed with advanced lung cancer. Amos flew to Germany to accompany his father for the biopsy, which confirmed that he had lung cancer. Amos's father was a life-long, heavy smoker, so the diagnosis did not come as a complete surprise. His father refused radiation treatment, chemotherapy or surgery as he did not want to prolong his life or have further pain. Amos had a family meeting with his father, mother and sister. His father expressed his wish to die at home without pain. He did not want to die, and was angry that he was dying. At the end, he refused to be shaved or bathed. He died in the Summer of 1999, within less than a year of the diagnosis. During that time period, his parents were supportive of each other and the family grew closer.

Amos recalled that his father had an unusual lifestyle, even in his later years, and that he tried to live life to its fullest up until his death. From the time Amos emigrated to the United States, his parents visited him once or twice a year. Initially they stayed with him in his apartment in Brooklyn, and then later stayed in his apartments in Manhattan. He insured that there was always a bedroom for them.

His father visited Amos by himself on several occasions. During those times, his father went with a relative to a casino in Atlantic City or in Las Vegas, or on the Chinatown buses that went to casinos. A few times he did not return until several days later, when he had been expected earlier. When he returned, finally, to Amos's apartment, he slept for two days straight. His father told him later that he had gambled away all of his money, that he did not have money for the bus back, and that he pushed himself on to the bus without paying by convincing the bus driver to take him back. When he arrived in Manhattan in Chinatown, he had no money for the subway. He jumped the turnstile several times, and at least once got lost on the subway. Once, when he emerged from the subway, he found himself in Harlem, in the early 1980's, when it was more dangerous there.

Amos's father talked to Amos about how he delighted in reliving his early life in Manhattan in the 1930's when he had visited from Germany. He was attracted to the "seedier" side of life where he could be with societal outsiders doing unconventional things. It was most comfortable for him to be on the "edge" either by virtue of the location, or activity, or both. Amos's father apparently relished going to "peep shows" on Broadway when he visited. Amos knew his father did that because he found plastic coins in the apartment from those shows. His father watched men playing three card monte in Times Square for hours, also, and spent time with people in that crowd. He took pleasure in going to Canal Street to buy fake designer watches and fake "bling." One of his favorite purchases was a heavy "gold" chain with a large lion head on it with fake diamonds as eyes. He frequently wore it.

Amos recalled taking trips with his parents when they were older as well. One trip was particularly memorable. They went to Amish country in Pennsylvania. Amos's father walked into the houses of the Amish where he was well received. They spoke in German together, although Amish German was not easy for them to understand. His father was curious about everything, talked to everyone, and took pleasure in having adventures. When he died, Amos felt the loss of his father's energy, vitality and spirit. He did not judge him for being the way he was. Amos's father was always a child, and rarely the responsible one.

After his father died, Amos travelled by himself to the funeral in Germany. While he was in Germany, he was on the telephone negotiating a deal to sell a website he had developed. When he returned home, during a four to six month period, he went on an ebay buying rampage. He bought items which he considered collectable, decoy fish and decoy ducks, at a cost of over $10,000.00. He had no idea why he went on that buying spree, but he recalled that it helped to numb his pain. In a sense, it was a different expression of his father's gambling. It was a way to gamble but with the justification that it was an investment. Amos could not speak about his father without getting tears in his eyes. He will always feel the pain of the loss of his father.

This was a pivotal time for Amos. Six months after his father died, his marriage ended after years of unsuccessful couple, group and individual therapy. His medical condition and the loss of his father made him feel, even more profoundly, that he had no time to waste to find more harmony in his life.

As for Amos's mother, a few years after Freddie's death, she moved to a pleasant apartment on the outskirts of Tel Aviv, Israel, to be close to her family, including one brother, and her best friend from concentration camp. She lived with a metapelet, a woman who cared for older people. She had a much closer, traditional family life in Israel, where she attended a continuous round of weddings, bar mitzvahs, funerals and other family events. She spent time with girlfriends at the Tel Aviv beach and elsewhere. She was content.

During the first five years that his mother was in Israel, there was the Second Intifada, which was a Palestinian uprising against Israel. In January of 2003, there had been a suicide bomb attack on the Tel Aviv Central Bus Station. Twenty-three people were killed. When Amos heard about the explosion, he contacted his mother as she lived about a mile away from the bus terminal. His mother told him that she heard the explosion. When Amos asked her if she felt safe in a country which was at war, she told him that he did not understand. She said that after forty eight years in Germany, she felt safe again. She told him that she could sleep at night, without one eye open, because she had all of her friends and family around her. Amos recalled that his mother had always given him the impression that she felt happy in Germany. This was the first time he heard her express her discontent with having lived in Germany for so long.

Amos's mother had always been a superb cook and had prided herself on that skill. Amos was in for another revelation. When he visited his mother in Israel in 2005, he was surprised that she had not cooked any dishes for him. She said she stopped cooking once Amos's father died. She told him she never liked to cook, and she only did it to please Amos and his father. Again, this was the first time that he heard his mother express such feelings. Was it old age talking, or was this how she always felt? It brings to mind the conclusion that we may never understand others, we may not even understand ourselves, and certainly time and aging may distort truths if there are any.

Amos's mother remained in Israel from about 2000-2008. She was adept at using a computer, despite her minimal formal education, and stayed in touch with family that way from the time that desktop computers first became popular, until the end of her life. She was among the first to use a computer regularly, and she played games, such as rummy, on it. She moved back to Germany, where Amos's sister and her family lived, after she developed metastasizing amelanotic melanoma, as the treatment for it was better in Germany at that time. Amos and his sister arranged for a beautiful apartment for her, and hired a Romanian caregiver who lived with her full time. Eventually, the melanoma worsened and she died in her home, as she always wanted to, with Amos and his sister present. Several weeks before his mother's death, Amos had a heart attack and had stents placed. When he heard that his mother was close to death, he made the trip to see her from New York against his cardiologist's recommendation. He was lucky that he was able to make the trip without any negative consequences regarding his health. He never regretted taking that risk in order to see his mother one last time. Her last words to him were, "Ah Amos, you are here."

# Chapter Nine: Amos's Years At An Ivy League Institution: 2001-2018

*"Faith is taking the first step even when
you don't see the whole staircase"*

—Martin Luther King Jr.

*"Work hard and become a leader;
be lazy and never succeed"*

—Proverbs 12:24

*"Small opportunities are often the beginning
of great enterprises"*

—Demosthenes

Two years after his father died, the newly appointed Chief at a major Ivy League medical institution in Manhattan approached Amos and offered him a part-time job, which he accepted. Due to Amos's medical condition, he was working part-time at the prior hospital. He was still recovering from his stroke, but he was improving. Amos believed that working for a major Ivy League medical institution, and for that Chief, would be rewarding and would enhance his career.

In the beginning, Amos performed jobs which he considered demeaning and below his capabilities, because they were responsibilities he had performed previously but thought he had outgrown when he was the director of the service. Initially, he was not involved in any lectures or research projects. He had to share an office, whereas previously he had his own, large director's office. He did not get the respect he previously had by virtue of his lesser position. Amos did not despair, as he always viewed things positively, and knew that he could do more once he was feeling physically stronger.

Despite his positive attitude, Amos faced another medical challenge. His second wife told him that he had a growth on his back. He could not see it because it was between his shoulder blades, in the middle, and he could not feel it. He went to a dermatologist who took a biopsy. It was diagnosed as skin cancer. The doctor performed an extensive surgery to remove the cancer and the surrounding tissue. It took the doctor significantly longer to remove the cancer because he was bleeding extensively. Amos was unable to change the dressing because of its location.

No matter what happened to Amos, he always went back to work right away, or he travelled. Rest was never part of the agenda, and he never allowed himself time to heal. About a week after the surgery, he travelled to Germany to visit his mother. While he was on the plane, he felt warmth between his shoulder blades. When he went to the bathroom, he saw that he was bleeding through the dressing. He took some underpants and put them between his shoulder blades, so that as he sat back in the seat, it would press against the wound. When he arrived in Germany, he went to a doctor immediately. The doctor told Amos that the wound had opened up. Each day he had to visit the doctor to change the dressing. By the end of that week, the wound was still open and clean. It eventually healed, although a large scar remained.

Amos summarized how he felt about that medical challenge with a story. There is a German fable about a hero called Siegfried in the Nibelungenlied, translated as The Song of the Nibelungs. Siegfried was a Prince who was known to kill a dragon. He bathed in the dragon's blood. While he was taking a bath in the blood, a leaf fell off of a tree and attached itself to the middle of his back between his shoulder blades. The dragon's blood protected his entire body except where the leaf had attached to his back. Eventually, someone found out about his vulnerable spot, and killed him. His wife had stitched across his shirt where he was vulnerable in the back, with a cross, and he was killed with a spear in that location. Amos felt vulnerable in the exact spot where Siegfried had his vulnerability. Amos felt vulnerable because of the cancer, because it was inaccessible to him, because he could not see or feel it, and because he knew that the scar was there forever. And yet, Amos appreciated that he had escaped the permanent consequences of danger again.

About three years into his tenure at the hospital, Amos realized that he had returned to over 90% of his physical capabilities, and he accepted a full time position as an ob/gyn. He took more "calls" and his salary was significantly increased. Shortly after he took the position, he received a telephone call from the hospital on his day off. There was a three day seminar training people on patient safety. There were train the trainer sessions, and the physician who was assigned to be trained had not attended that day. Amos was asked to attend the next two days of the training and Amos agreed as he knew that this would be an opportunity for him.

As a result of having taken that opportunity, Amos became the first ob/gyn in New York to become a team training trainer. His early involvement in theatre arts in Germany, and his Cologne-style sense of humor, helped to make him an effective and interesting trainer. He subsequently trained the entire department of over four hundred people, including physicians, nurses and others. He trained them on team training, which was learning how to be a team. The training was developed by the United States military and was also used in the aviation field. It was newly applied to the field of medicine. The Ivy League institution where Amos worked became the first in New York to train the entire department on team training. Today, it is a routine form of training in most hospitals.

Eventually, from that one telephone call, when he was offered the opportunity to attend a conference, Amos became a specialist in safety in obstetrics after much hard work. He developed new ways to make it safer to have a baby. It took many years to implement these safety measures at the hospital where Amos worked. His efforts were met with significant resistance, which led to more than a few requests to get Amos fired. He was not fired, because there was a realization by his Chairman and others that implementing safety measures, even against resistance, required a tough approach.

These methods were adopted by numerous other hospitals. The Ivy League institution where Amos worked prepared a major publication about their success, which was cited by many other organizations. It was cited, also, by malpractice lawyers, as well as by legal scholars, as the standard for making it safer to give birth in the United States.

During the first couple of years before the safety measures were fully implemented, the malpractice premiums at the hospital where Amos worked more than tripled. They then started to gradually drop to less than forty percent of what they used to be by virtue of the implementation of the safety measures. While up to fifty percent of all liability payments made by the hospital were for obstetrics, that number dropped to well below ten percent, which was exceedingly low considering that over twenty-two percent of admissions were obstetric patients and newborns. This was a great accomplishment as it has been the goal of modern obstetrics to make it safer to give birth to a baby and to prevent newborns and mothers from getting injured or from dying.

Amos wanted to return to his original, academic roots, and to start publishing more papers. In 2004 he had become the full-time Director of Labor and Delivery at a major hospital, and thus, making the time for it was difficult. Between 2001 and 2007, Amos published one paper. Amos determined that he would have to work at night and on weekends in order to accomplish his goal of doing more academic writing. Between 2007 and 2011, Amos published five papers which was about one per year. Between 2012 and 2017, Amos published an average of eight papers per year. He was able to increase the academic portion of his job because his Chairman encouraged him to do it, most of the papers were published with the Chairman, and he used personal time to write them. They wrote on the topics, mostly, of patient safety, ethics and a wide range of subjects involving home birth. In 2014, Amos was invited to dinner by his Chairman. At that dinner, he surprised Amos and told him that he had earned and would become a full professor of clinical obstetrics and gynecology. Amos never thought he would achieve that honor in his lifetime.

Other than Amos's parents, Amos felt that his Chairman was the most influential person in his life. He felt that his Chairman was helpful, supported him in what he wanted to do, gave him intelligent and positive feedback, and helped him to achieve his goal of becoming a full professor. Amos described their relationship as yin and yang in that they complemented each other and provided one another with a balance of intellect and emotions. They had opposite personalities. The Chairman was religious, traditional, quiet, calm and yet persistent with his academic work writing papers. He took his time making decisions and was gentle with people. The Chairman did not like controversy, and always looked for a peaceful solution. His maxim was, "be kind, be kind, be kind."

Amos, on the other hand, was a chronic multi-tasker, thought and spoke rapidly, made quick decisions after weighing all options, and was a change-maker. Amos could be hard on himself and others if mistakes were made, or change had not occurred quickly enough. He did not shy away from controversy and met it directly. Amos was not traditional and liked to be a maverick. The way in which their energies were the same is that both the Chairman and Amos were devoted to their work, and toiled hard to achieve their goals.

While Amos's "marriage" at the office was productive, supportive and life affirming, Amos had more difficulties in choosing a compatible mate in his private life. He re-married in 2002, and the marriage ended in divorce after eight years. The way in which they separated is of note due to the history of Amos's family of origin. Amos went with his then wife on a trip on a cruise ship. After bitter fighting at the beginning of the trip, Amos left the ship, while it was still docked, before the voyage commenced, without telling her. He went home, packed his things, and arranged for a rental apartment while she was still on the ship on the cruise. Amos recalled that his father had worked on a luxury passenger liner as a youth, which traveled between Nazi Germany and New York, and he kept returning to Nazi Germany. On each trip he spent several days in New York, but never escaped. Amos, on some cellular level, wanted to "jump ship" and escape what for him was an intolerable situation.

While this story is strange to many people, it is entirely consistent with Amos's personality. If he did not like a movie, concert or show, he left during intermission. If he did not like food he was eating, he threw it out. If he did not like clothing he bought, he gave it away. If he went to a restaurant and did not like the menu or ambience, he walked out before ordering. He would walk the streets and go in and out of many restaurants before he chose the one he wanted. If he went on a vacation, and did not like the hotel, he left. If he went to a social event, which he, in general, did not like to attend, and would rather be reading or watching television, he would find a place to do that during the event. He preferred traveling to places without having reservations so that he could decide where to go the last minute. He always wanted to keep his options open for maximum enjoyment. Perhaps this freedom to choose was an ultimate luxury for him given his parents' inability to choose so many things in their lives.

And yet, if Amos worked on an intellectual or other problem, either for work or for his website, he spent countless hours on it, at all hours of the day or night. He researched every aspect, and he persisted in finding the solution. He is someone who was and is exquisitely aware of how much time he has left, and how he wants to spend it. He has patience for what he is interested in. He lost all patience for doomed relationships which could not be made right, and in which he did not feel cherished, even after many years of trying. In 2011 Amos found a mate whom he described as the love of his life. Finally, his personal life is loving, stable and calm.

In the midst of these challenges and successes, Amos had another medical challenge. In 2010, as he was walking home from work on the East Side of Manhattan, through Central Park, to his apartment on the West Side, he felt short of breath and experienced pain. He could barely walk without stopping to take a breath. The next day, he had a cardiac catheter placed. Two vessels in his heart were found to be occluded, which means closed. Two cardiac stents were placed in his vessels. Amos was told that he had one heart attack shortly before the procedure, and one heart attack during the procedure. Amos considered this to be his other vulnerability. These medical events continued to propel Amos forward as he recognized that he might have limited time to do and accomplish all that he wanted to.

# Chapter Ten: Amos's Websites

"*Your time is limited, so don't waste it
living someone else's life*"

—Steve Jobs

"*Content is King*"

—Bill Gates

*A wise man will make more opportunities than he finds*"

—Francis Bacon

As mentioned earlier, after Amos had a significant stroke, in early 1996, he realized he had to find another outlet for his energies and for the medical knowledge he had accumulated over the decades. At that time, the internet was new, and Amos decided to "deposit his brain on the internet" so that in case his condition worsened, at the very least, his knowledge would be deposited permanently.

Amos needed to find a web designer to help him. Amos had volunteered at a Jewish soup kitchen at that time. There was a company in the same building as the soup kitchen, which designed websites. Amos met with people at that company, and explained to them what he wanted to accomplish. They quoted a price of about $4,000.00 at that time. Over the years, it cost Amos tens of thousands of dollars for the design. Although various individuals with large internet companies had offered to hire Amos to work on their websites, he wanted to be independent and not be an employee. Creating his own website was a better fit for him.

The web, at that time, was in its infancy with no content management systems ("CMS"). Every single page had to be created and coded separately. The URLs (uniform resource locator), a standardized naming convention for addressing documents accessible over the internet, were not as easy to identify as they are today. A URL at that time was for numbers, not words.

Amos sat down with the team to find an appropriate name for the website. They agreed on Babymagic. They then started developing a logo for the website. As the website was for women trying to get pregnant and for women who were pregnant, the logo they agreed upon was a rabbit with a top hat in his hand, pulling a baby out of the hat. Amos had always been a follower of magic shows and magicians, an area which fascinated him, so the logo was a combination of his interests and sense of humor. A couple of months later, Amos learned that the words Baby Magic in the United States were trademarked by a large company for baby oil. Because Amos was not born in the United States, the words Baby Magic were unknown to him. In reading about it later, he found out that the product Baby Magic and Amos were both born in the year 1950. Although there was some "magic" about that name, Amos had to change the website's name. He came up with Babydata. Several years later, the company that owned the trademark Baby Magic sued Amos to give them the name back, because Amos still owned the URL, Babymagic. After some back and forth negotiations, the company bought the name back from Amos for a nominal price.

While Amos was recovering from his stroke, he continued building Babydata. It was a very tedious process because it had to be done in small steps. He answered questions his patients had asked and he answered questions people had asked on the internet. Within less than three years, the site had grown to about 1500 pages, all created by Amos, including a few tools for women to calculate certain fertility and pregnancy data. The company he worked with helped with the tools.

Amos worked on the site mostly at night as that was the time that was quiet and he could concentrate on the website. At that time there was no money to be made on the internet. There were no advertisements yet and people did not make any revenue. It was not until the end of 1998 that Google was founded, which was two years after Amos created his website. Nonetheless, Amos continued to work tirelessly on building the website.

He was not worried about money during that time period because he was working part-time as an ob/gyn. In early 1999, one of his patients, who read his website, asked if her husband, who was a lawyer and was working on the internet, could take a closer look at Amos's website. Amos agreed, gave him access, and he informed Amos that Babydata was the fifth largest pregnancy website in the world. Amos had not looked at the statistics, so he did not realize that.

At that time, there was "internet craziness" as internet "traffic took off," and many people realized that the internet was something "big." The lawyer asked Amos if he was interested in selling his website. He offered to act as a broker. Amos had not realized that there was worth in websites at that time.

Amos agreed, and gave him a 40 percent commission, which, looking back, Amos said, was way too much. Amos did not expect to get any money from his website. Shortly thereafter, the lawyer found a company that bought Amos's website.

The money that Amos received from the sale of the website allowed him and his family to live more comfortably. Some of the money was given to Amos in stock, which was eventually transferred to another company and ultimately became worthless. At the time of the negotiations, Amos was in Germany for a shiva for his father. The timing adversely affected his negotiations as his heart was not in it during his grieving process.

About a year after the sale of Babydata, in 2000, Amos used some of the money he received from the sale to create a German website with the help of his sister, who lived in Germany. She translated the website from English into German, and helped with the design of it. Her husband worked on the website as a programmer. The German website was sold in 2003. Amos remained miffed at his sister because they had a verbal agreement to split all the proceeds equally. As the agreement was being negotiated with the buyer, she insisted that she get a higher percentage of the proceeds, of about seventy percent. At that time, Amos was financially comfortable whereas she was not. His mother somehow found out about their conflict and told him that since he had more money, he should give more to her. Amos felt that he was taken advantage of. His sister told him throughout the years that he was a bad businessman. Perhaps she was correct to the extent that business with family was problematic on a host of levels. Despite that conflict, Amos remained close to his sister due to his generous nature.

As part of the deal for the Babydata sale, Amos joined the company which bought Babydata. He became their internet website director for pregnancy and fertility. Amos performed that job from home. He answered questions from people trying to get pregnant and also from women who were already pregnant. He wrote a column several times a week on those subjects for the website. A year later the website that purchased Babydata was sold to WebMD and Amos worked for that company until approximately 2006, when he was offered a full time position at the hospital.

Once Amos stopped working with the internet company in 2006, he focused on a third website he had created called Babymed, which was based on a more updated internet technology. Amos wanted to create a website again because it was a creative outlet for him, and an innovative way to communicate with the world. He liked to make things, to be productive, to have people enjoy his productivity, to share knowledge, and to come up with different ideas. He jokingly said that the internet and his writings did not have a German accent. He felt that when he talked to people, his German accent could be distracting and abrasive. He also believed that his personality "shone through" better when he wrote content and developed tools. The internet was a comfortable place for him, too, because he was able to merge his mathematical ability with medicine. Dozens of the tools had complex mathematical formulas related to fertility and pregnancy, which people on the internet could use to personalize their experience. Amos enjoyed creating these tools with others more than anything else.

When Amos started creating his initial Babymed site, he hired a programmer who lived in the Midwest of the United States. They met in person twice even though they worked together for approximately seven years. They connected mostly through e-mails and on the telephone. The programmer was moody and difficult to work with, but what was most challenging is that he disappeared for long periods of time on many occasions without contacting Amos. The site was hosted on the programmer's home computer, which required constant attention. Finally, one time, when Amos could not reach the programmer, Amos took a trip to the Midwest to find him so that they could talk in person. Amos arrived in the airport in the Midwest, called the programmer, told him he was there, and said he would go to his house. The programmer suggested another meeting place, and they met in a dark, seedy bar. Several months later, after Amos found another more reliable developer, he fired the programmer.

Because Amos had been involved with the internet, almost from its inception, he had a perspective on its development. Amos had been fascinated by the changes over the last twenty years. In the late 1990's and early 2000's, the internet was in its infancy and technologically it was not easy to enter information and to present it. Initially, a website could not have pictures and different fonts easily. One could not organize content according to specific keywords and tags. Today, the content management system (CMS) is the "gold standard." It is much easier to use and allows for entry of information and presentation of information in a superior way. From its modest beginnings in the 1990's to today's website innovations and designs, Amos and his different websites moved along with the changes. It is now in at least the seventh iteration of website designs.

Presently, Babymed uses a CMS, content management system, called Drupal, which is among the most advanced of those systems. It has been the basis for Babymed since approximately 2010. Drupal allows content to be updated regularly across the entire website when web pages become outdated, and it removes duplicate pages. With Drupal, they can add modules that do several things such as weeding out spam users, and preventing people from registering as "bots," which is sophisticated crimeware.

Additionally, the website can be found by users more quickly. Drupal allows for much better search engine optimization ("SEO") of content so that people searching the internet find pages easier through keywords. On the back end, Drupal allows editors to edit pages better, and to format them so that the web pages are more pleasant and easier to read.

At the same time, the company Google, which Amos contended that most people know as a "box" where they find things on the internet, has helped people find the Babymed website. Amos stated that the vast majority of people using the internet are unaware that the search box is only a tiny percent of what Google actually does. Google, more importantly than anything else, sells advertising on the internet, and allows smaller websites such as Babymed to benefit from Google's success.

In the mid 2000's, Google started to implement an analytic system which made evaluation of websites, data and users much easier. Amos obtained, in real time, information about his users. Most importantly, he looked at the live website and saw how many users were on the website at that moment, and which pages they were on. That information made it easier to make necessary adjustments. Amos could track what kind of device people used to enter his website, which country they resided in, how they got to his site, what pages they were active on, and how many pages per second were being viewed. All of that information helped Amos figure out where to focus. Amos could see, also, the top keywords users used to find his website. For example, the top keywords used to find the Babymed website could have resulted in information on how to calculate the pregnancy month, the safety of certain medications, a menstruation calendar, information on whether masturbation caused lower sperm count, and the topic of missed abortion, which is a kind of miscarriage.

In order to access Google's analytic system, website owners like Amos placed a small code on their websites, and Google then, without charge, tracked internet usage including visits, page views, users, time spent on the site, and other significant information, as mentioned above. People who are experienced with mathematics and statistics, such as Amos, used that information to their advantage and improved their sites, which he does, regularly.

Whereas most people know that Google is a behemoth company on the internet, Amos maintained that only few realize what it actually does to be so successful. Google developed and used algorithms to identify websites. Each change on the algorithm improved or deteriorated the traffic to those websites. These algorithms included statistics, words, user data, quality of content, innovative content, and organization of content to identify websites that Google presented in better ways.

Over the last twenty years, the content for Babymed increased to approximately ten thousand pages. The number of tools expanded from about a dozen to six or seven times that many. Search engine optimization helped users worldwide to find pages on Babymed through over 10,000 keywords that show up among the top ten Google searches. Babymed is found in over one thousand searches in the top three ranks of key words. Its expenses are self-sustained by revenues which come from advertising. Babymed places advertising code on its website, and revenues are generated mostly from Google advertisements.

As originally intended, the information on Babymed helps couples to get pregnant and to have a healthy baby. What fascinates Amos about the internet is that there are always men and women interested in finding out about getting pregnant and being pregnant. There are few if any classes people can attend about getting pregnant. It is his hope that the Babymed website provides them with that information. One small but important feature on the Babymed website is a "fertility 101 course." There are over a dozen lessons teaching couples about the basics of getting pregnant and being pregnant. For example, when you enter into Google the keyword "fertility 101," Babymed is among the top sites that show up. The lessons provide the basics covering the time period prior to getting pregnant, the basics of getting pregnant, lessons on improving the chances of getting pregnant, and what to do about infertility once it is diagnosed.

The content on Babymed was based on the tens of thousands of questions that Amos has been asked on the internet, in his office, and in the hospital for the last forty years. Every time someone asked him a question, Amos answered that question extensively on his website. While it is rare today to get a question that has not been answered, Amos continues to add content to the website when someone asks a new question. Amos reviews the content on his website, creates a new page, and then answers that question in a way that enables people to find the information easily.

There are a wide range of questions which Amos has been asked on his website. The following are some typical questions. According to Amos, the simplest question is when a women states that she cannot get pregnant, and wants to know what to do. Some women tell Amos that their husband has a low sperm count, and they ask what that means and what they should do about it. Others tell Amos that their menstrual cycle is irregular and they want to know what that means, and what they should do about it. Some women tell Amos that they are on the pill, and they ask how they can know if they are fertile. Some ask if their sister had twins, or some other family member, will they have twins too. Another typical question consists of the woman providing her due date, and asking when she got pregnant. Some women tell Amos that their baby is not moving as much in utero, and ask if that is a problem.

The most popular tools on the Babymed website consist of the following. The website has a fertility calendar and calculator to figure out the woman's most fertile days and when she should have sex in order to get pregnant. Another tool is a test to determine an individual woman's chance of getting pregnant. The website has an interactive tool to help figure out whether the woman is pregnant based upon fifteen questions. One tool is a test to determine if certain symptoms mean that the woman is pregnant or not. An additional tool is a test to predict if the woman will give birth to a boy or a girl. The website has a pregnancy calendar to calculate the due date and other events including how many weeks pregnant the woman will be on which day.

While there are many other interactive tools on Amos's website, the overarching theme is that these interactive tools teach women about the important information they need to know when trying to get pregnant, and they teach knowledge women need once they become pregnant in order to have a healthy baby. For example, Amos stated that many women assume that all pregnant women have nausea and vomiting when they are pregnant, but the fact is that the majority of women who are pregnant will not have those symptoms and that those symptoms in and of themselves do not mean that a woman is pregnant.

What is truly remarkable about Amos's efforts is that, besides an eighty hour week at his job at the hospital, Amos has been the creator and the main content provider of Babymed for the last 20 years. He also has to oversee and manage other companies he hired to assist in his efforts. Initially, in early 2000, Amos worked with only one web developer who also hosted the site. As the internet changed, that person refused to change with the internet and make the changes. After four or five years, Amos had to work with companies. He hired his daughter and her friend, also, who worked on day-to-day efforts, for about four years.

There were several companies Amos hired to develop and program the site. There is also a company that is the host of the website and ensures that the website is stable and accessible to everyone around the world 24/7. If something is wrong with the server, that company guarantees that the site will be up and running from a different server within minutes. Amos was enamored with that web hosting company because they have substantial customers, including Al Jazeera, a media company. Additionally, in recent years, Amos has been helped by his business partner, and as of September 2017, a web consultant. The web consultant handles the day-to-day efforts which include checking the website to make certain it is stable, working on the design of the site, thinking of suggestions on how to improve the site, and managing the advertising.

What makes Babymed particularly unique and important is that it is the only website created and run by an obstetrician-gynecologist. Most of the other websites in the field are based purely on business models and are not run by physicians. Other sites hire physicians to write the content. Amos is one of the most experienced physicians in the world dealing with pregnancy and fertility issues. The language on the internet is different than the language a physician uses with patients in person or over the telephone. Amos is particularly skilled at conveying complicated information in terms which the public will understand, in a concise and precise manner, on the internet. For example, when Amos explains how to calculate the most fertile days to become pregnant, he boils it down to the five or six most fertile days to clarify to people that having sex every day will not necessarily improve chances of getting pregnant. While Amos has tried to interest many other obstetrician-gynecologists in getting involved in the internet, so far, they have not seen the value in it and have conveyed to Amos that they do not believe that it is time well spent. Amos was the first ob/gyn online doing that work, and he is still the most active online.

Amos has been a pioneer in understanding how people access information, and in changing with the times. In early 2010, Amos observed that there was a significant shift in how users view websites. Until about 2000, the majority of users accessed the internet through desktop computers. Over the last five to seven years, more and more users are using mobile devices, such as Smartphones and tablets, to access the internet. At the end of 2017, nearly nine out of ten users accessed Babymed through mobile phones, while less than ten percent accessed it from desktop computers. This fact came to many web developers as somewhat of a surprise.

It took some time for many sites to adjust to mobile access. Babymed was one of the first websites to become "mobile friendly." Babymed makes it easier for mobile users to calculate the data and to read information on the website. This access through mobiles is even more prominent in less developed countries outside the United States, where the vast majority of people access the internet through mobiles and not with desktop computers.

Amos recognized that as more and more users use the internet, the trend of people searching for medical issues will continue. While there are many other websites informing people about medical issues, the topics of getting pregnant and pregnancy remain among the top issues people search for. Therefore, because of its long life on the internet and its continuous updates and improvements, Babymed is well positioned to provide this information.

As far as the future goals of Babymed, Amos is determined to be persistent and consistent in helping to improve the site and in making needed improvements to remain competitive, such as improving mobile access. Amos is determined not to "burn through" money that is being invested in the website, but to spend money wisely within revenues. That will prevent Babymed from making changes that eventually turn out to be "losers."

Amos stated that it is relatively unknown what the internet will look like five years from now. He was reminded of a quote from Yogi Berra, the famous baseball player, "[i]t is tough to make predictions, especially about the future." He opined that "everybody in this business is trying to make these predictions, and billions of dollars are spent and invested in sites that people believe make the right predictions, however, many of these will eventually fail. Even 'smart money' is not that smart."

One of Amos's biggest challenges is to continually improve and change the information on the website to make it up-to-date and medically relevant. According to Amos, every five to ten years, half of the medical information changes. Printed books, for example, have long development cycles. In many cases, by the time they are published, much of the information is already outdated.

The development of the internet, and Amos's participation in it over the last twenty years, has intrigued Amos. It helped to heal him from his stroke and it gave him a strong, additional purpose in life. After decades of practicing medicine, Amos felt that his internet work was healthy for his brain, and it provided stimulation and an outlet for his prodigious intellect and energies. It was also an extension of his academic work in teaching, training and publishing. The internet audience, however, remains different and limitless. It is different because people have a shorter attention span while viewing the internet, and Amos cannot see people's faces. Thus, his communication has to be shorter, clearer and to the point. It is limitless because Amos's writings can be viewed on the internet throughout the world.

# Chapter Eleven:
## Amos's Patents

*"Science knows no country, because knowledge belongs to humanity, and is the torch which illuminates the world"*

—Louis Pasteur

*"Do or do not, there is no try"*

—Yoda

Amos's career has been about combining the knowledge he gained in his profession, with creative ways to spread the information to all communities. He created, also, tools and products to enhance the information. While many of the tools on the Babymed website are unique, and could have been made into patents, Amos did not have the time to pursue those, and now that they have been in use for many years, they cannot be made into patents anymore.

However, earlier in Amos's career, he did develop some inventions. These inventions evolved from his schooling in Germany. While he was in medical school in the early 1970's, Amos attended several classes on natural medicine and herbal medicine which were part of the required curriculum. He took classes, also, on meditation and on medical massage. When Amos arrived in the United States for his residency program, he soon learned that herbal medicine and natural medicine were not accepted topics in medical education in the United States. However, approximately one hundred years ago osteopathic medicine, with its reliance on alternative medicine, was taught in medical schools in the United States. It was Amos's view that alternative medicine was important for physicians to consider in that they should be knowledgeable about every aspect of treatment that could potentially improve a patient's physical and mental health.

After Amos suffered a stroke in 1996, and while developing his website, he recalled what he had learned in German medical school about herbal medicine. He began to read books from Germany about herbal and natural medicine, especially as it related to fertility and pregnancy. Amos was surprised to learn that the leading brands of pregnancy vitamins taken by nearly all women in the United States contained artificial dyes which were considered to be carcinogenic. These dyes were added by major pharmaceutical companies to improve the appearance of the vitamins and had nothing to do with improving their efficacy.

After several years of research, Amos decided to develop a supplement that included fertility enhancing herbs. In addition to the vitamins, Amos researched which herbs were found to improve fertility for the women's formula, and also for the men's formula. Women and men could take their respective supplements prior to conceiving to improve their fertility and the health of the pregnancy.

In order to achieve this goal, in the early 2000's, Amos approached a small company which at that time sold pregnancy tests online. Amos knew of that company because they bought advertising on Amos's website. Amos convinced them to work with him on developing these supplements and several other items to help couples get pregnant, or which would help women during pregnancy. At that time, they were a tiny company. Today, the company has revenues that exceed well over ten million dollars. It took years to develop the correct formulas.

Amos named the supplements FertilAid, which were developed for both women and men. He also developed other natural items to help couples get pregnant. Eventually, Amos licensed those supplements to the company. Amos and the company applied together for patents, which they received, for female and male enhancement supplements. His inventions were visionary as it has become clear that male and female infertility has become a major problem internationally. Without the internet, the success of these supplements would have been impossible. Amos hired a top United States research university to do peer reviewed studies of the supplements.

Interestingly, over the last years, FertilAid for men has approached and exceeded sales of FertilAid for women. There are now scientific peer reviewed studies which show that the product improves sperm count. This has become crucial, as over the last decades sperm counts all over the world have declined, which makes it less likely for men to have fertile sperm counts. Nobody knows definitively why sperm counts are down. It may have to do with the warming of the atmosphere or the exposure of men to toxic substances. Amos was ahead of his time again, as his development of a male fertility supplement became ever more important over time. Men are an important part of the fertility equation, and one of the goals of Amos's website was to teach men to check their sperm count first if there were difficulties getting pregnant.

Fertility and pregnancy are the topics which Amos learned about for decades. He disseminated information and created products using his knowledge. After 1990, in vitro fertilization ("IVF") became more and more popular. While Amos was not a reproductive endocrinologist, he found out that while many couples spent tens of thousands of dollars on IVF, they could save that money by first trying to improve their own fertility through life changes and supplements. Life changes included eating healthier foods, losing weight, getting the proper amount of exercise, and having sex regularly and in a timely fashion when they were most fertile.

Amos's success has been in acquiring useful knowledge to help people, and then communicating that knowledge from the widest platform, with whatever tools he could develop. Clearly, his inventions are part of that success.

# Chapter Twelve: Safety and the Home Birth Debate

> *"Perhaps this is the moment*
> *for which you have been created"*
>
> —Esther 4:14

> *"As my family planted for me,*
> *so do I plant for my children"*
>
> —Talmud

> *"Whoever saves a life saves the world"*
>
> —Talmud

Amos has had success in numerous endeavors. Around 2006, Amos began to work on research and papers with the Chairman of his Department. Over time, Amos attributed more and more meaning to that form of communication. At first, he started writing papers on the topic of patient safety. He chronicled the work they had conducted on making deliveries safer for women and their babies. The initial paper was the first one

in the United States to show that making significant improvements through educational efforts, policies, and collaborative
practices in the labor and delivery context could make a significantly positive impact on safety.

That paper was not well received by the hospital or the
obstetrician groups despite the fact that it showed that tight-
ening up rules and ensuring that policies were uniform could
improve outcomes. Such groups did not want to tell obstetricians what was right or wrong in clear language, and instead
preferred to leave policies and recommendations vague. Amos
was disappointed by that reaction as he expected that they
would want to establish uniform policies which would improve outcomes. Instead, they continued to recommend more
vague and general recommendations. The only groups which
were extremely enthusiastic about the paper were malpractice
lawyers for plaintiffs.

Many years later, and after other publications, more
people began to realize that having uniform, clearcut, simple
and straightforward guidelines would be the best way to improve safe outcomes in hospitals. Amos helped to develop such
guidelines. Despite this change in opinion, it became a nearly
daily struggle for Amos to maintain the guidelines in the hospital where he worked because doctors continually found reasons to bypass the guidelines and to do things "their own way."
Amos was contacted regularly by doctors, nurses, residents and
administrators who requested to do things differently and less
safely than set forth in the guidelines. Amos often had to over-
rule them to keep them within tight and uniform guidelines
which better ensured safety.

What Amos experienced in the hospital setting is similar
to what had occurred in the motor vehicle industry with safety.
It took decades to implement the requirements of safety belts,

car seats for children, and airbags in cars. The car industry had been fighting against safety regulations and recommendations until the laws forced them to implement them. Today, lives are being saved on a daily basis with the enforcement of these laws.

It was Amos's belief that if hospitals and obstetricians would implement safety requirements routinely, lives would be saved on labor and delivery. He was correct. Positive results from the implementation of the tight guidelines at the hospital where Amos worked occurred earlier than expected. There were significant decreases in liability insurance premiums. Prior to the implementation of these guidelines, about one in two dollars spent on liability in the hospital went to obstetrics, while obstetrical patients were only one in four of all patients. Over the years, as of 2017, less than ten percent of liability expenses went to obstetrical issues. In addition, liability premiums had decreased by over sixty percent, saving the department of obstetrics and gynecology over three million dollars per year, and saving the hospital tens of millions of dollars per year.

Another example of changes to improve safety which Amos was a part of included the development of a uniform protocol to induce labor with oxytocin and written guidelines for communication and chains of command. Amos led team trainings for everyone on this topic. Amos also did simulations to address such issues as bleeding and shoulder dystocia, where the shoulder of the baby became stuck in the pelvis after delivery of the baby's head. They hired a nurse whose sole responsibility was safety. All of these efforts resulted in increased safety.

After Amos and his Chairman published several papers on patient safety, they next focused on safety regarding home births. In 2009-2010, there had been a significant increase in home births in the United States. Home births increased by five to ten percent per year. As of 2017, the United States had the largest total number of home births in the developed world. Amos's research focused on accessing the Center for Disease Control database which was the largest database in the world. It was easily accessible online, and he used it to publish well over ten publications on home birth outcomes. That database collected over 110 data points for each United States delivery, which was culled from birth certificate data. A data point is a field which includes such things as the state the delivery took place in, a mother's age, a baby's weight, and the outcome.

In the papers which Amos and his Chairman published on home birth, they compared the outcomes of home birth deliveries with the outcomes of deliveries in the hospital. What they found is that significantly more newborns died during home birth compared to hospital births. They found, also, that significantly more newborns had neurological problems after home births compared to hospital births. The causes of those bad outcomes were that babies who were delivered during home births were more likely to have oxygen deprivation issues, presumably because they were not monitored appropriately during labor. At home births, fetal monitoring was not available, and if a newborn was born with an issue, there were no personnel available to resuscitate the newborn.

During their research, they discovered, too, that in the United States, there was a group of women who performed home births. They called themselves midwives, but they had not received typical midwife training. In the United States, typical midwives would commence their education with a nursing degree, then work as a nurse for some time, and then attend an accredited midwifery school. During that time, the nurse would receive an advanced degree before or while attending midwifery school. After finishing midwifery school, the midwife would become licensed and certified as a certified nurse midwife.

However, in the United States, most of the women who performed the majority of the home births called themselves certified professional midwives, when in fact they were not. The requirements for becoming a certified professional midwife were at a minimum a high school degree and an online course observing twenty-five to fifty deliveries at home. They did not have any academic training, and rarely if ever worked in a hospital where they would have been exposed to hundreds of deliveries. Amos maintained that being exposed to only a few dozen deliveries before becoming an independent practitioner was completely insufficient to understand the potential complications of deliveries. Amos recalled that he needed thousands of deliveries to learn the potential complications which could occur and how to best manage them. Moreover, Amos contended that all women, including low risk women, should give birth closer to operating rooms where any emergencies could be taken care of more efficiently.

Amos maintained that women desiring all natural childbirth could deliver in a hospital birth center. He helped to create two such centers in New York City. Both are still in existence. Amos helped to develop strict protocols for these birth centers to insure that only low risk patients were being taken care of there, and to make certain that the nurse midwives in these units followed proper protocols. There was a third birth center in New York City which had to close because they had less clear safety guidelines and the deliveries were inappropriately supervised. Eventually, there were too many bad outcomes for the mothers and babies, and too many malpractice suits against that birth center. Amos firmly believed that this example shows that safety for women in labor can be ensured only with education and with strict adherence to uniform guidelines.

During the time period that these papers were published on home birth, Amos and his Chairman were regularly attacked by home birth midwives, especially after they published a paper explaining why these so-called midwives were "unprofessional." These papers expressed firmly that from an ethical point of view, every woman who considered home birth must get informed consent which should include clear information about the increase in adverse outcomes with home birth. Moreover, these papers argued that because of these adverse outcomes, any professional must recommend against a home birth and should not attend a home birth so as not to participate in a situation where there are increased complications. The topics of other papers Amos worked on included relatively adverse outcomes from home births as opposed to hospital births with regard to newborn survival, neurological outcomes, apgar scores, and oxygen deprivation.

There were attacks against the ideas promulgated in these papers. Some people argued that a woman's autonomy should allow her to decide on home birth on her own, and that the recommendations against home birth and attending a home birth impinged upon a woman's autonomy. Amos contended that these recommendations strengthened a woman's autonomy, and that it was a part of feminist empowerment for women to get recommendations based on facts. Amos considered it unethical to omit important information when discussing home birth. Amos's views were borne not only from his research, but also from his observations over decades. Many women and babies were transferred to the hospital with significant complications after home births, which could have been prevented if they had delivered in the hospital.

Prior to the first publication on the subject, in 2013, Amos attended a conference at the Institute of Medicine in Washington, D.C., where the subject of home birth was being discussed. His Chairman presented the draft of their very first paper. The majority of the audience consisted of home birth midwives. They interrupted the Chairman's presentation so that he was unable to finish it.

Ironically, Amos was, and remains, very supportive of appropriately trained certified midwives. As part of his training as a resident and fellow, Amos was trained extensively by certified nurse midwives. He learned to value their philosophy and their approach to deliveries, as their approach is more natural and less interventional. He relished working with them. When he found out about the "rogue" midwives in the United States, who did not have the appropriate training, and who conducted the births at home, he felt he needed to get involved and to help to inform the American public about what was truly going on. Amos believed that vulnerable pregnant women get "abused" by "rogue" midwives who talk them into something that has such a significantly increased risk. He wanted to expose this deception. In general, Amos was fond of midwifery practice, to the point that his residents called Amos's labor and delivery coverage "midwifery day" because he introduced them to a different approach on how to safely deliver a baby. Again, Amos was willing to stand up for what he believed in, against negative comments and attacks from different quarters.

As of early 2018, the Center for Disease Control birth data shows a significant slowing down of home births. Between 2015 and 2016 the number of home births has remained essentially the same. This may be due to the publications of Amos and his Chairman informing women interested in home birth that they may be more dangerous than previously believed.

# Chapter Thirteen:
# Ethical Issues

*"Ethics is nothing else than reverence for life"*
—Albert Schweitzer

As Amos discussed themes in his life, the topic of ethics kept emerging. It has been a lifelong struggle for Amos to parse out what is right from wrong in different contexts. He continually thought deeply about ethics both in his private life and in his profession. He had an overarching need to get things "right" in every context, and to behave ethically. He wanted to be a "mensch," a person of integrity and honor.

He described his life growing up in Germany as all about day-to-day survival. His father never had a paying job. His mother took care of him and his sister to the best of her ability. Women at that time, in that society, did not work for the most part. Initially, he lived in a tiny room with his family, and then in an impoverished neighborhood in a one bedroom apartment in the early years. The family had to get through the day even though they had no money. Nobody in his family did anything overtly illegal to survive, Amos contended. What they did do in order to make their lives easier was to "whitewash" things. They denied to themselves and to each other that certain negative things were happening. They also told each other white lies and did not discuss issues. They never discussed anything in their lives as a real problem. Amos's father had a serious gambling addiction. The family never discussed that as being a problem. It was only later in life that Amos realized that his father's post traumatic stress disorder and gambling addiction had a significantly negative effect on their stability and on their lives.

While Amos was growing up, there was often little food in the house. Nonetheless, they had a small dog. His father went to the butcher regularly with the dog in his arm and asked for bones with meat on them for the dog. He brought the bones home, and his mother used them to make soup for the family. Despite this, as a child, Amos maintained that he felt richer than everyone else because his parents always had a lot of friends who visited them, and with whom they had good relationships. They had friends in the neighborhood, across town and abroad.

Amos's father had his own set of ethics which was different from Amos's mother's and from Amos's standards. They did not criticize his father for this, but they were not capable of doing the same things. Amos's father was a photographer. He made money by going to the many commercial exhibits in Cologne, and taking pictures of politicians visiting the hall and of the stands of the various companies exhibiting there. In order to work as a photographer in those halls, he was supposed to have a license as a photographer and he was supposed to belong to a photography union. He never got a license and never joined a union. Amos's father did not believe in "organized anything." He did not want to follow the German rules for trades, and he did not want to go to the authorities to apply for a license. Nevertheless, he continued to work in the hall for decades, and was well known there.

When Amos asked his father why he never applied for a license, he told him that he did not believe in organized trades. He told Amos continuously that he would have died, "many times over," if he had always done things according to the rules. Amos's father wanted Amos to be different, however, and to have a chance at leading a better life with a good job and more money.

Amos's father's refusal to follow rules extended to other contexts. Amos's father refused to buy tickets to events. He did not want to be part of the system, and always found a way around it. At these events, he oftentimes walked around the building until he found a side entrance and snuck in. Amos was sometimes with him when he did this. One time, when Amos was a child, there was a guard at the entrance. Amos's father told Amos to lift a cable with him that was on the ground, as if they were performing a job, and to keep stepping to the right until the cable took them into the entrance without paying for the tickets. Amos's father always tried to live life outside the norm. He told Amos that he thought that people who bought tickets were stupid.

Amos knew from an early age that many things his father did were not "ethical," but he could not judge him for it because of what his father had endured. Even though Amos's father made some money every year, he never filed a tax return in Germany in fifty years as he did not believe in taxes. His primary belief was that Germany owed him, not the other way around.

Amos's father's dubious ethical decisions sometimes were made in order to be generous to Amos. There was a six day indoor bicycle race in Cologne each year around New Year's day. A team of two bicyclists raced around an oval without interruption for that period of time. Amos's father attended the race every year to take pictures of people, and to take pictures of people with the famous bicyclists. Amos still has some of the photographs. Amos attended the race with his father from the time he was six years old. There were different themes for the bicycle race, including a segment where the bicyclists would race, and whoever won that race would get a child's bicycle to give to one of the thousands of children who were lining the arena. Each year, Amos would get that bicycle. Amos thought that it was because he was cute, or screamed the loudest, or pushed himself in front of everyone else. For many years, he was the happiest boy in the auditorium. It was only several decades later that it dawned on Amos that perhaps he did not get those bicycles "legally." When he asked his father about this, his father smirked but did not answer.

Amos's father "gamed" the system in other ways. Every year there was one race where the winning bicyclist was given a car. Ford Motor Company had its European headquarters in Cologne. They donated a car every year to the bicycle race. Each year, Amos's father would drive home with that car. They had a new car for the whole year, until the following year, when he got a new car and sold the older one. Again, Amos did not know how that happened. Years later, his father admitted that he bought the car from the bicyclist each year with cash, and sold the year old one elsewhere for a moderate profit.

Years later, when Amos was living in New York, his parents visited him annually. Amos took his father and mother to many restaurants, and always left a tip on the table as was customary. After many years, Amos's father admitted to Amos that he took the tip off of the table each time and kept it, as he thought it was superfluous and unnecessary. Amos's response was to laugh, as he knew that this action came out of his father's sense of necessity, rather than his being mean or selfish.

Amos recalled that other family members sometimes brought new ethical questions into Amos's world. Sometime in the 1980's, Amos's cousin's husband arrived in Germany. Amos's father agreed to drive the cousin's husband to a northern German city at his request as he claimed he had business there. Amos's father drove him to a dock where they built ships. About a half an hour later, the husband came out with a heavy suitcase. Amos's father drove him back to Cologne, and they did not talk about it. Amos's father later looked in the suitcase, and found that it was filled with hundred dollar bills. The cousin's husband, when asked about it, told Amos's father that it was money for a Brazilian General. The General was to be given that money by a German Company after he decided to have the German Company build several submarines for the Brazilian Navy. The cousin's husband was supposedly a supplier of weapons to the Brazilian Army and Navy at that time. At no time did Amos's father think that this was an illegal transaction. Amos thought it was a bribe and argued with his father. Amos's father told him that he was extremely fortunate to have found a job that allowed him to be above the law, where he did not have to do anything illegal to survive. He told Amos that he should not criticize others for having to engage in certain activities to survive.

This same cousin divorced, and then married an American doctor who did not work as a doctor at that point. Her taste in men was tragic, or perhaps her desire for riches clouded her better judgment. Around 2003, the cousin and her second husband visited Amos in New York. The second husband told Amos that he owned several websites. They sold medications to people on the websites. Amos asked which medications. He told Amos that they were medications people needed for such conditions as high blood pressure and diabetes, and that because he sold them on the internet, he could provide those medications for less money. He told Amos that he employed doctors who worked for the website. The customers interested in buying medications would fill out a health form. The doctors would review the forms, follow up with patients if needed, and would then prescribe them the medications. The website was working with pharmacies all around the United States which would supply medications at a reduced price.

He asked Amos if he was interested in becoming one of those doctors. He told Amos that it would be easy. All he would need to do is review the medical forms. If he felt uncomfortable, he would not write a prescription. If he felt comfortable, he would write a prescription and send it to the pharmacy where patients would pick up the medications. He told Amos the payment would be $50.00 for each prescription and that he could do about one hundred per day, seven days per week. Amos did not feel comfortable writing a prescription without seeing a patient, and he declined the offer. The entire scheme did not sound ethical to Amos, and was "too good to be true." About a year later, the second husband was arrested by the FBI and convicted under the RICO Act for distributing drugs. They confiscated his five houses and ten cars, and they found eighteen million dollars in cash in the bank. He had paid taxes on that income, and maintained that his activities were within the law. That incident confirmed for Amos, again, that doing something illegal was never worth it.

During Amos's career, he was offered many opportunities to make more money when it was not completely legal, but he always declined them. His strong desire to do things differently from his father and others whom he had observed over the years sometimes caused him to lose patients. Some patients had asked him to write notes which were not true in order to get time off from work, or to extend sick leave, or for other reasons. When Amos refused to write the notes, some of these patients would leave him. His ethical sensibility would not allow him to do it.

Amos believed that although his ethics were tested many times, his ethics had in fact improved over time. Until his daughter was born, he felt that his ethical compass was incomplete. He remembered that when he was in Germany, as a young man, he had a car in which the starter did not work. When it was time to sell the car, he did not divulge that fact to the buyer, and he kept the engine on the entire time while showing it. The buyer did not realize that the starter did not work. Amos still felt guilty about that incident. He mentioned, also, the example of when he looked over at another student's paper, whom he did not know, at the Connecticut medical licensing examination, and expressed regret that he did that.

When his daughter was in middle school, Amos attended an ethics class at her school. They discussed a hypothetical situation. A person was buying something in a store, and received change back that was larger than it should have been. The class was asked what their response would be. At that time, the answer was not obvious to Amos. In his world, if a mistake was made by another person, it was their fault, and if you profited from that error there was no problem with that. Amos supported keeping the money. He realized, after some discussion, that this was not the correct ethical answer. They did not teach ethics in Germany. Amos's father had his own set of ethics. His loyalty to his father, and his own sensibilities, probably given to him by his mother, made ethical questions confusing for him. What was also confusing for Amos is that everyone he grew up with, at one point or another, did different things that were not within the law.

Although Amos does not have a particular view on the ethics of committing suicide, unfortunately he had seven close friends from Germany who committed suicide at different times in Amos's life. When Amos discussed those suicides, he was understandably upset, even all these years later. He wished he could have helped them. He wished that he and they could have been more open about what they were feeling at that time. Amos believed that it is ethical to support people and to talk with them when they are suicidal.

It was unusual for Amos to have known so many people who committed suicide with whom he was close. He could not explain why this was so. Perhaps it was because he was strong and competent. Troubled people were drawn to him. He was used to helping people as he had supported his parents and sister throughout the years. He also grew up in a time when there was a lot of experimentation with drugs and alcohol. Amos and his friends considered themselves to be outcasts because of their politics, their families, and the way they grew up. His friends rejected their families because they were more intellectual and had a different set of values than their families did, and, hence, they were not close to them. Perhaps what saved Amos from a different fate was the fact that he was close to his family, and because of his positive temperament. Also, despite some minor experimentation with risky behavior, he was unlike his father in fundamental ways.

Amos described what had happened to some of his friends. Amos was close friends with one man, Klaus, from the time they were teenagers. As teenagers, they did some risky things together such as jumping in front of trains, and jumping back just in time as the train approached. Amos was comfortable with some degree of risk taking as his father encouraged living "on the edge." Klaus was drafted into the army, and when he returned, he entered medical school. Amos had already completed some years of medical school because he had not been drafted as he had flat feet. Klaus was challenged by the demands of medical school. Amos learned one day that Klaus had been admitted to the hospital because of an overdose of pills during his second year of medical school. Amos visited him in the hospital. He told Amos that he had done something stupid, that he had been "stressed out" from school, and that he would be fine. Klaus's family, who were blue collar Christian Germans, were not warm to Klaus or to anyone else, according to Amos, so Klaus did not have much support from that quarter.

About three months later, Amos received a phone call. He heard that Klaus shot himself in the head and died. When Amos inquired what had happened, Klaus's girlfriend told Amos that she had witnessed the incident. She and Klaus were in the basement room of another friend, and they had an old fashioned hand gun with two chambers for two bullets. They started to play Russian Roulette, which is a game of chance in which a player places a single round in a revolver, spins the cylinder, and then places the muzzle against his or her head and pulls the trigger. Klaus held the gun against his head, clicked it, and it had an empty chamber. He clicked it again knowing that the next chamber had a bullet in it, and died instantly. Some years later, Amos learned that Klaus's girlfriend's brother committed suicide by shooting himself in the head on a different, subsequent occasion.

Ironically, another friend of Amos and Klaus, who witnessed the incident with Klaus, also died a few years later.

While Amos was in medical school, he had a semester of forensic medicine. As part of the course, he went to the Institute
of Forensic Medicine where people who had died under questionable circumstances were examined. On one occasion, he
saw the body of that friend. Amos had lost contact with him,
and was naturally quote shocked to learn of his death that way.
Apparently his friend had hung himself the day prior. Unfortunately, it was not just that group of friends who were doomed.

Around that same time, Amos became friendly with a
slightly older student in medical school. He was active in left
wing politics, and had created a collective to care for runaway
children. His wife also worked at the collective, and she became
pregnant. After delivery, she developed postpartum depression.
During that time, Amos's mother took care of her baby while
she recuperated in the psychiatric unit. Several years later, she
had a second pregnancy, she developed postpartum depression
again, and Amos's parents cared for the newborn until the
parents' families took over. Amos's friend and his wife named
the second newborn after Amos's mother. That time, the wife
refused to be admitted to the psychiatric unit for her depression. One day she disappeared, and could not be found. Many
months later, her body was found in the woods. Amos's mother
told Amos that she had gone into the woods with a can filled
with gasoline, and she incinerated herself.

Tragedy was never far away from Amos or from the
friends he chose, and who chose him. In medical school, and
afterwards, Amos traveled with his closest friend, Tom, many
times, including a six week trip to Turkey. They went to pubs
in Cologne, watched movies together, and shared many happy
times with mutual friends. Tom took hard drugs and drank
heavily in medical school and afterwards, habits Amos did not
share. Tom reminded Amos of his father because of his risky

behaviors. Amos continued to stay in close touch with him over the years. He became a general practitioner. Tom visited Amos in New York, and Amos visited him in Cologne.

In 1986, Amos had a long telephone conversation with Tom. He told Amos about his troubles at home and at work. He was trying to change his life. He and his girlfriend were about to move to one of the Canary Islands in Spain for a job. One week later, Amos received a telephone call from a mutual friend that Tom had hung himself in his apartment. They found syringes in his apartment. It was likely that he was drug addicted. Amos recalled that Tom committed suicide shortly after the World Cup final in soccer when the German team lost to the Argentinian team. In Germany, soccer was all and everything. The whole population became elated or depressed based on the outcomes of soccer matches. Amos thought to himself, as a joke to take away the pain of the loss, that Tom committed suicide because Germany lost the soccer final.

Amos had some ethical quandaries with another kind of suicide, assisted suicide. After Tom died, there was an issue with one of his sister's closest friends who was an artist. He developed ALS, amyotrophic lateral sclerosis, also known as Lou Gehrig's Disease. It is a progressive neurological disease that causes the neurons that control voluntary muscles to degenerate. As his condition deteriorated, he asked Amos if Amos would help him to die. He wanted Amos to travel to Germany where he lived and supply him with some medications. Amos was not comfortable doing that. Several years later, Amos's sister told him that her friend had died. Amos learned that one person had started an intravenous solution to kill him, and after he died, another person came and removed it so that there were no signs of what happened. Amos did not specifically refuse to help him, but it turned out that other people took care of it for him.

More misfortune struck Amos's old friends. In the late 2000's, Amos received a telephone call from his mother. She told him that one of his best friends from his teenage years, Wolfgang, who lived across the street from Amos's family, was found dead in the basement of his house by his wife. Wolfgang was the brother of the girlfriend of Klaus who had witnessed Klaus's suicide. He had married a Palestinian woman and had three children with her. They were all friends with Amos's mother. Although his wife would not admit that he committed suicide, Amos's mother was told by Wolfgang's mother that it was a suicide. It was never officially declared a suicide. Wolfgang was a physician and the head of a neurologic institute. He had taken care of Amos's father several times prior to his father's death. Although Amos does not remember signs of his being troubled when they were teenagers, Amos learned that he had become a drug addict and alcoholic. Although Wolfgang was a German Christian, he was considered an outcast because of whom he married.

As it turned out, Amos was one of the few of his group of close friends from Germany who was not drug or alcohol addicted. Amos explained that he was extremely afraid of drugs and of losing control of himself. More than anything, he wanted to succeed in life. He wanted not only to keep his head above water, but to rise higher. It was just "in him." Other than his own will, his ambitions originated from his desire to please his parents. It hurt Amos deeply that his parents came from miserable life experiences during their time in concentration camps. Amos felt that it was his utmost duty to improve their lives financially and emotionally. He felt that his success would help to accomplish that.

His friends did not share the same drive to live and to succeed, nor did they absorb the lesson of discipline in German culture. Some were not as street smart as Amos. Amos had more determination to move ahead, also. Amos was able to look at the bigger picture and to look years ahead. He was willing to make sacrifices in his day to day work in order to achieve something. When Amos created his websites, he believed that he had a good chance to be successful. Nobody was helping him originally because there was no short term benefit. Others could not see that there was a future in it. Perhaps because of having been educated in Germany, he had a certain kind of discipline that helped him to achieve his goals.

Amos did not know why his friends who were raised in Germany, who committed suicide, did not get the same message. Amos had more family support than others on a certain level. His father continually talked to him and told him that while he himself had considered committing suicide many times, he ultimately decided it was not worth it and that there were so many ways to enjoy life. Amos's father wanted to commit suicide in the concentration camp, and later in the 1960's. When Amos was ten, he was not aware of it, but his father was treated several times in a psychiatric sanatorium for many weeks. Amos was told a white lie at the time, that his father had to be reevaluated for his health pension. Perhaps knowing that his father had the will to live even after all that he had been through helped Amos to survive and to thrive on some level.

Amos did not leave catastrophic events behind him in Germany. When he was a first year resident in ob/gyn in the United States, he had a friend who was also a first year resident, but his residency was in anesthesia. They connected because Amos had previously done a residency in anesthesia in

Germany and in New York. One day, Amos learned that staff at the hospital found his friend dead in the doctor's locker room, apparently from a drug overdose. Amos did not know that he had a substance abuse problem, and was in shock. The cumulative effect of these types of events had an effect upon Amos, but he remained strong and productive.

Several years after that death, Amos's then best friend Ken, who was a year behind him in the ob/gyn residency, telephoned Amos. Ken had slurred speech. Amos went to his apartment and found him slumped on the couch, barely breathing or talking. Amos drove him to the emergency room of a different hospital and spent the day with him while he was being detoxed. Several months later, a similar incident happened again. Then, a third time, Amos saw him at the hospital and he had slurred speech. Amos reported him to the Chairman, who arranged for Ken to go to a drug treatment program. Ken was not angry with Amos for reporting him, and on some level was grateful to Amos for having saved his life several times. After Amos helped him to be accepted into a prestigious maternal-fetal medicine fellowship the following year, as he was smart and hard working, Ken had to drop out soon after because it was too stressful for him. Eventually Ken and his girlfriend moved to another state, where he practiced medicine. Amos learned that on Amos's birthday, in 2014, Ken's license to practice medicine was summarily suspended as he failed to cooperate and did not attend the hearing. They wanted to evaluate his physical and mental condition. He was found guilty of professional misconduct, and New York took away his license too.

In trying to understand why Amos had many close friends with mental issues and substance abuse problems, while there is no simple conclusion, part of it has to do with

Amos's impulse not to run away from trouble, but to run towards it and to try to make a difference. He tried with his father, and that pattern continued throughout his life. He found people with problems to be interesting and worth spending time with. If the people in his world were not in crisis, it did not feel "normal" for him.

# Chapter Fourteen: Lessons Learned from Amos's Parents

*"But let justice roll on like a river,*
*righteousness like a never-failing stream"*

—Book of Amos 5:24

*"Let us rise up and be thankful, for if we didn't learn a*
*lot today, at least we learned a little, and if we didn't*
*learn a little, at least we didn't get sick, and if we got*
*sick, at least we didn't die; so let us all be thankful."*

—Buddha

Amos's life has been one with many challenges, but with an overarching theme of positivity. Many of the lessons his parents were able to teach him, and which he was open to adopting and building upon, are inspiring, especially because of what his parents experienced. Hope in the face of horror.

One of the best lessons Amos learned was that of perseverance. He was taught to never give up. For example, when Amos applied to medical school, he was initially rejected. His father met with the Dean and convinced him to accept Amos.

Once Amos was accepted, Amos made certain that he became one of the best students, and later, a top doctor. He made the most of the opportunity. Amos was taught to learn something every day, to never rest on his success, to keep moving, and not to stay home to wither.

The lesson of the importance of education was imprinted upon Amos by his parents. He was told that he should teach his children good values, including that of the importance of education. While his parents did not have much education, no matter how little money they had, they always made sure that there was enough to buy Amos and his sister the books they needed for school. Amos's father taught him the importance of reading and learning. He told Amos that it was not important how much knowledge you had in your head, but that what was important was knowing how to obtain the information. He taught him that the same principles apply to many other aspects of life. For example, his father told him that it is was not important how much money you have in the bank as long as you have the money when you need it. Amos recalled that one year, when he was nine or ten years old, he was supposed to attend a Jewish camp. The bill had not been paid. His father went out that night to take photographs in pubs so that the next day, at 9:00 a.m. when the train departed, he would be able to pay the fee before Amos left on the train. And he did.

Amos has continued to read, research and write throughout his life. Higher education, and Amos's temperament, allowed him to earn more than his father, and to save money, which his father was never able to do. Amos made it a point to avoid last minute crises in his personal and professional life by planning well and by being disciplined.

Another lesson was to forge ahead for what you believe in, and if you are not successful one way, try a different way and be flexible. He was taught to be creative as survival requires creativity. Amos's father never became a licensed photographer, as he did not want to apply for the license from the German authorities. Nonetheless, he worked for about forty years as a photographer, and was accepted in the exhibition halls and elsewhere such that he made it work on his own terms. When Amos had his stroke, and thought he might not be able to work as an ob/gyn again, he learned everything he could about the internet, and started his own website to share his knowledge and to continue to be productive. As he recovered, he went from working part-time as an ob/gyn, to full time, and continued with his website work, wrote books, published articles, trained doctors and hospital personnel, and found many ways to share his talents. He did not let his health issues defeat him, and was flexible with his work activities based upon his health.

Amos was taught to advocate for his beliefs. When Amos learned about the problems with inadequately trained midwives and home births, he worked with his Chairman on research and published articles to expose the issues, and to make things safer for women and babies. He stood up to opposition and remained strong. With his work to make hospital practices safer, he had to forge ahead against stiff opposition there too.

Most recently, when Amos was in Vienna, Austria at the medical school, he saw a photograph of one of the former Chairmen on the hallway wall, in a place of honor. He was Chairman from 1938-1945, and was a known Nazi SS Officer. When Amos asked a member of the administration if he would remove that Chairman's photograph, he at first received opposition. Amos was told that the SS Nazi Chairman, who had taken the apartment of a Jewish doctor who was sent to concentration camp, had made many fine contributions to women's health and that Amos was only seeing one side of the story. Amos contacted other more powerful people in that administration, persisted, and the photograph is no longer hanging on the wall. In its place is a picture of a green tree, which is the translation of Amos's last name from German to English. That result would never have happened without Amos's tenacity.

Additionally, Amos's parents taught him to be fearless. He was taught to not shy away from confrontation. They told him not to confront others, but that if he was confronted, he must find a way to respond to the situation in a way that was non-confrontational but conveyed to others that he was aware of what was going on. He was told that he must show them that he was strong enough not to let them "walk over" him. Amos's mother exhibited to Amos that she could be fearless when needed. One day, Amos's mother learned that his sister had been arrested and was being held by the police on charges that she had harbored a member of the Baader Meinhof group. That was a terrorist group which was active in Germany in the late 1960's and 1970's. Amos's mother went to the police station and talked to the police with the goal of getting his sister released. Amos maintained that she spoke with the police so long and forcefully that they finally released her. She told the police that she was a survivor, that it was painful to see her daughter imprisoned falsely, and that they must release her. They did. Amos observed that his parents persevered and convinced people of things without offending or threatening them. They made other people feel safe. If Amos's mother had an idea in her head, Amos recalled, she pursued it in her own quiet way, and often prevailed.

His parents taught him, also, not to trumpet his intentions. They advised him to diplomatically pursue his goals, and not to prematurely celebrate, but only to tell people of his successes after they had been achieved. They counseled that this would prevent people from undermining him earlier in the process.

His parents, however, taught him contrary lessons when it came to dealing with authority. His mother always tried to follow the law and customs. His father, on the other hand, did not believe in authority. His father did not believe in following the law when the law prevented him from doing something he wanted to do. His father taught him not to follow rules blindly, and that sometimes he might have to break the rules in order to survive and to preserve his dignity. For instance, Amos's father never stood on lines, he never paid an entrance fee or bought a ticket to any event, and he never paid taxes. He engaged in "innovative thinking" when it came to outwitting authority. He taught Amos that if he had followed the law, he would have never survived the concentration camps and his other experiences. When he was starving and homeless when he arrived in Israel, his father went into people's homes on Yom Kippur, while they were in synagogue, and took their food.

Amos respected his father's cunning on a certain level as a survival mechanism, but inherited his mother's respect for and adherence to laws and regulations. In fact, Amos's enforcement of rules and regulations as an administrator at hospitals reflected his adoption of the lessons he learned from his mother and from the German schools and culture. And yet, there is a bit of a maverick in Amos, which is more of his father's influence.

Amos's mother, in particular, taught him certain basic life skills. She counseled him to always be punctual. She taught him to wake up every morning with all of his strength as his spirits must be high for each new day. She told him that early morning rising was important. She said it was the best time for him to achieve his goals as he had the most energy then. In advising Amos of this, she recalled that when she was in the concentration camp, if she arrived at the smelting oven first, to do her job, she was able to choose her most convenient place to work.

While Amos's father could not hold onto money because of his gambling addiction, Amos's mother taught Amos to save money. She saved money in a tin can and was always hiding money. She told him that if he had money left over from whatever he did, he should put it away and forget about it. If he needed the money later, he would have it to use. She taught him that he should always keep enough food at home and to save food, too, so that he would have it in times of scarcity. She believed that survival depended on behaving like a squirrel. She counseled that he should be patient when waiting on line, as it is impossible to know whether being further ahead is better. She had learned this from the concentration camp lines. Perhaps it was a larger message that being patient allowed one to evaluate all options.

Amos's father taught him basic hygiene lessons when he was a young boy, which exemplify a larger life attitude. For instance, he taught Amos to always wear clean underwear. When Amos's father was in the British Army in Palestine, as a soldier, he was always expected to dress neatly. He told Amos that the leaders only looked at how you appeared on the outside, but nobody cared what you looked like under the uniform and did not care if you were clean. Amos's father told him it was important to be neat inside and outside. He stressed that Amos needed to take care of himself and should not worry only about outward appearances. Later in life, the general importance of cleanliness continued to be relevant in the hospital and in the practice of medicine. And, with all of Amos's medical conditions, self care remained an important lesson.

Another lesson Amos learned from his parents was the value of spontaneity. It was the norm in Amos's family to do things that were pleasurable in a spontaneous manner. When Amos lived with his parents as a young person, it was not unusual for his father to wake up in the middle of the week, to tell Amos that they were going to Paris, for example, and for Amos to find himself one half hour later in a car on his way there. Since his father never had a regular, steady job, such outings were possible. They never made any reservations in hotels, and would drop by any place they wanted, even if it took hours and hours to find a hotel room that they preferred and which they could afford. Amos said there were never any bad feelings about this, as spontaneity trumped excessive planning. To this day, Amos will change reservations on a moment's notice, look for a restaurant or hotel for hours, and travel without reservations. He is used to changing his mind, living for the moment, and dealing with uncertainty. And yet, he is more disciplined than his father, and more of a planner, such that he has done a lot of research before engaging in spontaneous events. Clearly, Amos's version of spontaneity is a modified version of his father's.

His parents taught him to have a positive attitude about other people. He was told not to assume that everybody is mean, that there are "good souls" in the world, and that by finding them, his happiness will increase. Given the many betrayals his parents suffered in their lives, it was a philosophy borne out of hope. They also told him that he did not have to be religious in order to have a productive and enjoyable life.

Although saved for last, perhaps the value which Amos's parents held most dear was to help others in need. They taught Amos that there are always other people who are "worse off" than he. They told him not to withhold money or love from others. As a family, they all had access to the same accounts and money, and were allowed to take money when needed, but they had to act responsibly. Amos's parents, even though they had few resources, shared their food and housing with others when needed, and helped them financially if they could. Amos has done the same. Throughout Amos's life he has supported his family members and others financially and emotionally, far beyond what most people have done or have been expected to do.

# Chapter Fifteen: The Impact of Being a Second Generation Holocaust Survivor

*"Whoever listens to a witness, becomes a witness."*

—Elie Wiesel

*"We must always take sides. Neutrality helps the oppressor, never the victim. Silence encourages the tormentor, never the tormented. Sometimes we must interfere. When human lives are endangered, when human dignity is in jeopardy, national borders and sensitivities become irrelevant. Wherever men or women are persecuted because of their race, religion, or political views, that place must— at that moment—become the center of the universe."*

—Elie Wiesel

Many scholars have written about the impact of the Holocaust on the children of survivors, the second generation. In examining Amos's life, I tried to examine that issue as it applied to him. I spent many hours interviewing Amos and listened closely to his stories about his family and the trajectory of his life. I asked him many questions, many of which he had not considered answering before, and that he had tried not to think about. After learning about his life and how he made sense of what happened to his family, and to him, and after observing him closely, I concluded that pieces of what he had to say applied to others similarly situated, but just as much was like a snowflake and unique to him and his family. I read much of the massive literature on the effects of the Holocaust on second generation holocaust survivors, but determined that an emphasis on comparisons with Amos's experience would do a disservice to the uniqueness of Amos and his family.

Amos did not like to read about second generation survivors. He felt that the books and articles on the topic often portrayed the second generation as more traumatized than not. He did not want to look at himself as if he were a victim. He rejected the idea that he was traumatized in any respect.

With regard to survivors, one theory was that only the tougher ones survived because they were able to disregard ordinary standards of morality. Henry Kissinger, a former United States Secretary of State, was a Jewish refugee who fled Nazi Germany with his family in 1938. He was quoted as saying, "[o]ne had to survive through lies, tricks and by somehow acquiring food to fill one's belly." Amos said that Kissinger's description was that of Amos's father's behavior, who taught him his survival techniques.

The literature on Holocaust survivors often stated that many survivors "look better" from the sociological point of view than from the psychiatric one. Research found that more survivors stayed married, and that four out of five survivors married other survivors. Also, research indicated that survivors were particularly concerned with their children and that survivors, more than others, tended to be overprotective parents. In Amos's case, while his mother initially had post traumatic stress disorder, she was able to overcome it, largely. His father, however, suffered from it all of his life. They remained married despite many challenges. However, they were not overprotective parents. If anything, they had a laissez-faire style of parenting and left Amos and his sister largely to themselves on a day-to-day basis. They wanted them to obtain their own experiences, and were more akin to bohemian parents in their approach. They did intervene when support was needed, but that occurred relatively infrequently.

It has been stated, also, that survivors and their families have a widespread ability to think quickly, to size up situations, to break down complex elements, and to make intelligent decisions. Amos stated that he did those things his whole life, almost as a matter of instinct.

Like many Jewish parents who were not survivors, Amos's parents always wanted him to "further himself." His parents' emphasis on education is what helped Amos to transcend his circumstances. Perhaps Amos's ambition was enhanced by his wanting to please them and to make them happy and proud of him after all they had suffered. He was competitive by nature as well. And, his parents did everything in their power to make certain he succeeded in school. When he did not do well in gymnasium academically, his parents encouraged him by getting him tutors. His mother prepared breakfast for him every morning and made certain that he arrived at school on time. Since his mother was not educated in the academic sense, it was difficult for her to understand what was required. The same was true for his father. Amos recalled that he did not truly commence academic learning until his first year at medical school. Before that he felt that he did not know how to learn or to write quality papers. Nobody in his family, or with whom he was close, had finished university. The majority of students he went to gymnasium with did not attend university. Less than one in ten of the students were intellectuals. Most of them went into business. Some went into the arts. In his milieu, the other parents were less interested in their children in the academic sense. Amos's parents were more focused on Amos "getting ahead" and achieving goals that they were not able to reach for themselves.

Amos's father, in particular, felt that his own dreams had been thwarted. He told Amos that he wanted to be a lawyer or doctor, but that he could not accomplish either dream because of the Nazis. He told Amos that Amos was responsible to fulfill his dream. Amos did not feel burdened by that responsibility. His father was willing to do everything in his power to help him with this, including helping to get him into medical school by advocating with the Dean. For Amos's father, a career in law or medicine was not about making money or being in business. He wanted Amos to help people in a humanistic way. Even when his father wanted him to be a lawyer, it was not to become a commercial lawyer, but to fight injustice with legal skills.

While Amos was growing up, he stated that he never looked at his parents as being survivors or as being different. They were always a close family unit and he never compared his family to others. He was more focused on looking inwards, toward his own family. In addition, his family was extremely social. They had many, many sleepover guests, and they were integrated into their own society. Amos did not feel lonely or isolated, even though his father considered himself and his friends outcasts. When Amos emigrated to the United States, he was interviewed by a researcher about his German/Jewish upbringing. The only physical manifestation he could recall is that while he was growing up in Germany, he always had constipation. The only time he did not have it was when he went to Jewish camp. This is significant because he did not recall any emotional manifestation of having been raised in Germany as the only Jewish boy among seven hundred students. While that is hard to believe, Amos's strong denial mechanisms, and his whitewashing of problems, both survival techniques learned from his parents, made his statements plausible. Those techniques overpowered any of his sensitivities. His body was not immune from the stresses, however.

In looking at Amos's adult behaviors, some of them seem to be the emotional manifestations of having been a second generation Holocaust survivor. He was morbid at times, and preoccupied with death, deformity, and disease. He bought a lot of food, and made certain that his home was always overly stocked. His mother taught him to save food in case of times of scarcity. He joked that he emigrated to New York City so that he could read the New York Times every day. He made certain that he read the news multiple times a day, and had emergency news alerts on his phone. His parents counseled him that he must be sensitive to political changes, and must be ready to flee when necessary. His parents advised him that possessions are not everything, that he has to be ready to give them up, and he must remain on the alert to get rid of things in an emergency. His parents told him to keep cash on hand in case of an emergency and to buy gold coins. His parents emphasized that part of success in life is to make enough money to have a comfortable life, but they were not focused on having a lot of money. He was attentive to any fluctuations in the financial markets. He made sure that his accounts and passwords had maximum protections. He was concerned with safety, and made certain that his home was outfitted with smoke alarms and other detectors at all times. Thus, all things considered, he was perhaps more vigilant in trying to keep his world safe than others who have taken safety for granted, and who did not have parents who were stripped of their safety and comforts in so brutal a fashion.

When Amos met people, he told them about his background immediately, including many stories about what his parents went through in the concentration camps. In his own mind, those experiences clearly defined him in a significant way. He said that he did this because most people he met in this Country grew up in a comfortable, middle class life. He felt that people needed to know where he came from so that they could understand who he was. It was not political for him, but purely personal.

His life in New York was more akin to that of other immigrants. He had less financially as a child, but felt that he had a better life in many ways than others who had more resources who grew up in the United States. He had to support his parents financially throughout his adult life, and sent them money on a regular basis. He spoke with a heavy accent, which he felt made it more difficult to advance in this society. His thinking, he believed, was more German than American in that his tendency was to look at the micro level, the details. He believed that Germans were more focused on precision and clarity than Americans. He stated that he has learned to look more at the macro level, the overall picture, since he emigrated to New York. Since English was not his first language, he had difficulty understanding typical American idioms which he believed sometimes resulted in communication issues. His integration into society in New York was not challenging because he was a second generation Holocaust survivor, necessarily, but because he was an immigrant who had to make many adjustments.

Amos had certain sensitivities which may or may not be related to the fact that he was a second generation Holocaust survivor. He described that he had a radar for people who cheated, lied and were insincere and did not let them get away with it, especially at work. He attacked and exposed them. When he felt that people behaved incorrectly, he went into "high gear" and wanted to insure that they understood that they were not doing the right thing. Perhaps his reactions, at times, were more extreme because of his background. He had a strong sense of justice from his parents. Many times he chose not to be diplomatic if the people were "nasty." He maintained that he would be diplomatic if people were kind and it would hurt them not to be. He observed people hurt others, and he was not tolerant of that. His mother instilled in him the importance of kindness and generosity.

Amos was concerned with punctuality and efficiency, which he attributed to his German background. Sometimes he could be too hard on himself and others when things did not run smoothly in any aspect of his life. In that sense, he could sometimes be perceived as being difficult. He felt that he worked effectively and in a rational way so in that sense harder than some others. He was not afraid of taking on a lot of responsibilities. He was not afraid of taking on new tasks and learning new skills. He did not run away from difficult situations or people. He liked to run things, to control things, and to be in charge. He preferred to be the hammer rather than the anvil. Those traits helped to insure his success. Because of his dedication and closeness to his family, his focus and discipline, his intellect, his sense of humor, and his innate disposition, he did not suffer the fate of some of his friends who became drug and alcohol addicted and suicidal. Quite the contrary. Whether his successes had anything to do with being a second generation Holocaust survivor has been difficult to discern. His family background certainly contributed to giving him drive, purpose, and street smarts. His Israeli origins made him tough. His German training gave him structure, discipline and work ethic. His assimilation into New York life made him flexible. The combination has made him unstoppable.

# *Afterword*

"It is not the strongest of the species that survives, nor the most
intelligent, but rather the one most adaptable to change"

—Charles Darwin

After hearing all of the family stories and thinking deeply
about what Amos's life and that of his family represents, from
a societal, political, personal and psychological standpoint,
what remains most striking are the lessons they teach all of
us, by example, about survival. But not just about mere survival. It is about making the most of whatever situation they
found themselves in. They were adaptable in that they were
able to adjust to new situations. They learned new languages,
they assimilated into various cultures, and even were adept at
technology in later years. They valued education. They were
resourceful, flexible, persevering, and fearless. They remained
hopeful. They did not let bitterness overtake them.

They were capable of gratitude for the small, everyday
things. They could still see the beauty in the world, whether
through the lens of a camera or in cooking a meal. They allowed themselves joy even when they struggled to remain op-
timistic. They were able to forget, and to whitewash what they

could not forget. And yet, they valued remembering their lost families and what happened to Jews and others in War II. They were proud of themselves, of being Jews, although they were not religious. They had self-respect. They were able to "fit in," while still retaining their individuality. They were not overly materialistic. They cared about people, and had big hearts and an attraction for outcasts and the downtrodden. They were generous and valued family, friends, travel and adventure. They were forgiving about each other's faults. They supported and tried to help one another with whatever resources they each had, although Amos had the role of a parent, often, even as a young child.

This view of Amos's family is based upon what he presented. While there may be more negative sides to all of it, that is not what he retained in his memories. And, true to his family ethos, and their way of seeing the world, he continues to see them in an almost purely positive way. Amos, a second generation Holocaust survivor, learned these family lessons well. For him, his survival depended upon his leaving Germany, where he felt that he would be hindered professionally. He also needed some separation from the intensity of his immediate family and their implicit and explicit demands upon him. What he inherited from his parents, in large measure, is his adaptability and his strong and compelling life force. You feel his energy when he walks into a room. He wants to take on responsibility. He wants to run things. He wants to take over, to control, and to show you how you can do things in a better way. He has a large measure of self-confidence and swagger. He has a strong sense of justice. He does not mind working harder, longer or doing the dirty work. He never forgets where he came from, and he wants others to know about it too. He wants to share his knowledge, to improve systems, to make things better for people. He seeks attention and wants to be acknowledged for his work. His vehicles, thus far, have been medicine and technology. He has an artistic side, a "good eye," and is proficient at photography and cooking, interests of his parents.

While a stickler for punctuality, efficiency and protocols, rules and regulations, he also tries to live spontaneously, with an element of surprise and fun. He has travelled extensively throughout the world, and continues to do so. Despite many health challenges, and two failed marriages, he always looks ahead in a positive manner. He expresses that he has so much to accomplish, and that he may not live long enough to do everything he would like to do.

I call Amos my lucky penny because of his sunny attitude. So does the cleaning lady at the hospital where Amos works because he gives her pennies and other change he finds on the floor, as a joke between them. He has a habit of finding money on the ground and passing it on. The truth about Amos is he has made his own luck. Admittedly, he had the advantages of a superior intellect and, in some ways, a supportive early family life. He knew he was loved. Later on he had mentors along the way, especially his Chairman. But, unlike many others, he made the most of those advantages. And, he has overcome the challenges of traumatized parents, poverty, his own ill health, divorces, the loss of family to the Holocaust and the loss of many friends to suicide. For him, one of the Ten Commandments in the Hebrew Bible, "[h]onor thy father and thy mother," has been a guiding principle, and has made him stronger every day.

# *Acknowledgements*

I wish to express my gratitude to Amos for the endless hours he spent allowing me to interview him and to probe his psyche. He did so with his characteristic generosity, although it was not an easy task for him. I am also grateful to Laurence B. McCullough, Debra Lynn Mechanick, and Rae Ellen Vitiello for taking the time to read the book and for giving intelligent and helpful suggestions and edits.

I am profoundly appreciative of this opportunity to share these inspirational stories of survival as a tribute to Amos and his family, to keep their memories alive, and on a more global scale, to keep the memories of the Holocaust and its aftermath alive.

# About the Author

Susan L. Pollet resides in New York City, and loves to write, to make art, to travel, and to have adventures. She has a life partner, several daughters, a grandson and a granddaughter. In 2018, Susan was the Shortlist Winner of the Adelaide Literary Award. Susan has been a lawyer for forty years, primarily in the area of family law. Ms. Pollet is a 1979 graduate of Emory University School of Law and a 1976 graduate of Cornell University. She graduated as a member of two honorary societies, and has published over sixty articles on varied legal topics in the New York Law Journal and law reviews in the area of family, criminal and domestic violence law. She has participated in multiple legal education training programs as an organizer, speaker and moderator, and taught college law courses. Susan has been active in the women's movement for decades as a chair of multiple committees and as President of the Westchester Women's Bar Association ("WWBA"), and as Vice President of the Women's Bar Association of the State of New York. Ms. Pollet is a recipient of the Joseph F. Gagliardi Award for Excellence, given to a non-judicial employee of the Unified Court System in the Ninth Judicial District for "distinguished service, devotion to duty and the administration of justice, and for outstanding service to the public." She is a recipient of the Marilyn Menge Award for Service, given to a member of the Women's Bar Association of the State of New York for "valuable and significant contributions to a chapter or to the statewide organization." She also served as Executive Director of Pace Women's Justice Center, whose mission is to eradicate domestic violence and to further the legal rights of women, children and the elderly through the skillful and innovative use of the law. She served as the Director of the New York State Parent Education and Awareness Program, which was designed to help separating or divorcing parents better understand the effects of their breakup on their children and to give them information and ideas about how to make the new family situation easier and more livable for themselves and their children. She worked on special projects for the Office of Court Administration. She also served as a lawyer for children, a court attorney to a judge, and as a prosecutor and a grants administrator. For the past eighteen years she has been the Archive and Historian Chair for the WWBA, which includes providing a monthly interview in its newsletter of judges and lawyers. She has a strong desire to provide the public with information about interesting people's lives who give us all hope. *Lessons in Survival: All About Amos* continues her work in that vein.

Printed in Poland
by Amazon Fulfillment
Poland Sp. z o.o., Wrocław